A Family Treasury of Little Golden Books

A FAMILY TREASURY OF LITTLE GOLDEN BOOKS

46 BEST-LOVED STORIES

Selected and Edited by
ELLEN LEWIS BUELL

Introduction by LEONARD S. MARCUS

The cover and endpaper designs are by Feodor Rojankovsky

GOLDEN BOOKS • NEW YORK
Golden Books Publishing Company, Inc., New York, New York 10106

Library of Congress Catalogue Card Number: 98-84343
ISBN: 0-307-16850-6 A MCMXCVIII

CONTENTS

INTRODUCTION

IN THE FALL OF 1942, a bold publishing experiment was launched with the happy goal of making high-quality children's books affordable, as never before, to the average American family. Little Golden Books were an immediate and resounding success. Introduced in wartime, the cheery well-illustrated volumes became a bright spot on the homefront and standard issue during the baby-boom years that followed.

The experiment began as a partnership between Simon & Schuster—upstart publisher of mass-market Pocket Books and crossword collections—and the Western Printing and Lithographing Company, whose giant presses, for reasons of cost, had to be kept running constantly. To drum up new business, Western's subsidiary, the Artists & Writers Guild, helped develop book ideas for a variety of publishers. The Little Golden Library was to prove far and away the Guild's most ambitious venture. In 1942, in a nation with more than ten million small children, a picture book typically appeared in an edition of five to ten thousand copies, and sold at $1.75. In a dramatic departure from this pattern, Little Golden Books rolled off the presses in editions of fifty thousand and sold for a quarter. In less than a year, despite wartime shortages, Simon & Schuster shipped a phenomenal 2.7 million Little Golden Books to stores, and had back-orders for another two million copies.

It was not just the twenty-five-cent price that was right. The sturdy, colorful books appealed to plain-spoken Americans' unfussy sense of fun—and of themselves. *The Poky Little Puppy* and *Tawny Scrawny Lion* added fresh and lasting comic heroes to the picture-book pantheon. *Seven Little Postmen* and *A Year in the City* celebrated industrial-age know-how while touching on the universal themes of children's curiosity and need to feel at home in the world. *Tootle* underscored the bedrock value of stick-to-itiveness in the single-minded manner that can be comforting to children. For anyone who doubted the educational value of books that cost so little, each bright little volume bore the endorsement of "Mary Reed, Ph.D., Assistant Professor of Education, Teachers College, Columbia University."

The series did have its detractors. Prominent librarians dismissed the Little Golden Library—unfairly, on the whole—as subliterary and market-driven. Tonier bookstores sometimes refused to stock the twenty-five-cent volumes. Demand for the books nonetheless proved so great that an unprecedented number and variety of sales outlets soon carried them, including book- and department stores, five-and-dimes, drugstores, and supermarkets. By the 1950s, Little Golden Books shared shelf and table space with the latest issues of *National Geographic* and *Life* in millions of American homes.

As this *Treasury*, consisting of forty-six Little Golden Books published between 1942 and 1957, makes plain, a stable of gifted writers helped create the early lists. Georges Duplaix made his mark not only as an author. As production manager of the Artists & Writers Guild, Duplaix was also one of the Little Golden Library's visionary planners. Jane Werner Watson (who wrote for children under more than a half-dozen names) doubled as the Guild's editor. Dorothy Kunhardt's credits included one of the most popular children's books ever published, *Pat the Bunny*. Phyllis McGinley wrote light verse for the *New Yorker*. Bank Street School founder Lucy Sprague Mitchell was a leading proponent of books for the very young. Among Mitchell's students at Bank Street were Edith Thacher Hurd, Ruth Krauss, and Margaret Wise Brown, all of whom went on to write books that have become classics.

The impressive roster of Golden illustrators was a notably international group. Hungarian satirical artist Tibor Gergely had fled occupied Europe for New York in 1939. Russian illustrator Feodor Rojankovsky resettled in the States two years later, his passage paid for by Georges Duplaix. Garth Williams came over from London during the Blitz. Swedish artist Gustaf Tenggren arrived via the Disney Studios, where he had art-directed *Snow White*. Alice and Martin Provensen, the latter also a Disney veteran, made their picture-book debut with *The Color Kittens*. Another new talent on the Golden list was the young and soon to be *very* busy Richard Scarry.

The present volume was first published as *A Treasury of Little Golden Books* in 1960 by another Western subsidiary, the Golden Press. It was the children's book review editor from the *New York Times,* Ellen Lewis Buell, who made the selections. In the book's original foreword, Buell expressed her delight at the prospect of giving a "more enduring form" to "certain" Little Golden Books—approximately one in ten of those published—that she herself found memorable and that the children she knew had "read to tatters." How has the *Treasury* held up since 1960? On the whole, very well. Readers today will surely wince at the caricatured depiction of African tribesmen in an illustration from *Pets for Peter*. Contemporary children will wonder why only the father in *Daddies* goes off to work. These examples, on view in the pages that follow, are reflections of another time and can and should be discussed. They are the bathwater that comes with the baby—this beaming *Treasury,* a joyful, time-tested, history-making collection of writing and art for children.

—Leonard S. Marcus

A FAMILY TREASURY OF LITTLE GOLDEN BOOKS

THE POKY LITTLE PUPPY

By JANETTE SEBRING LOWREY

Illustrated by

GUSTAF TENGGREN

Five little puppies dug a hole under the fence and went for a walk in the wide, wide world.

Through the meadow they went, down the road, over the bridge, across the green grass, and up the hill, one after the other.

And when they got to the top of the hill, they counted themselves: one, two, three, four. One little puppy wasn't there.

"Now where in the world is that poky little puppy?" they wondered. For he certainly wasn't on top of the hill.

He wasn't going down the other side. The only thing they could see going down was a fuzzy caterpillar.

He wasn't coming up this side. The only thing they could see coming up was a quick green lizard.

But when they looked down at the grassy place near the bottom of the hill, there he was, running round and round, his nose to the ground.

"What is he doing?" the four little puppies asked one another. And down they went to see, roly-poly, pell-mell, tumble-bumble, till they came to the green grass; and there they stopped short.

"What in the world are you doing?" they asked.

"I smell something!" said the poky little puppy.

Then the four little puppies began to sniff, and they smelled it, too.

"Rice pudding!" they said.

And home they went, as fast as they could go, over the bridge, up the road, through the meadow, and under the fence. And there, sure enough, was dinner waiting for them, with rice pudding for dessert.

But their mother was greatly displeased. "So you're the little puppies who dig holes under fences!" she said. "No rice pudding tonight!" And she made them go straight to bed.

But the poky little puppy came home after everyone was sound asleep.

He ate up the rice pudding and crawled into bed as happy as a lark.

The next morning someone had filled the hole and put up a sign. The sign said:

BUT.....

The five little puppies dug a hole under the fence, just the same, and went for a walk in the wide, wide world.

Through the meadow they went, down the road, over the bridge, across the green grass, and up the hill, two and two. And when they got to the top of the hill, they counted themselves: one, two, three, four. One little puppy wasn't there.

"Now where in the world is that poky little puppy?" they wondered. For he certainly wasn't on top of the hill.

He wasn't going down the other side. The only thing they could see going down was a big black spider.

He wasn't coming up this side. The only thing they could see coming up was a brown hop-toad.

But when they looked down at the grassy place near the bottom of the hill, there was the poky little puppy, sitting still as a stone, with his head on one side and his ears cocked up.

"What is he doing?" the four little puppies asked one another. And down they went to see, roly-poly, pell-mell, tumble-bumble, till they came to the green grass; and there they stopped short.

"What in the world are you doing?" they asked.

"I hear something!" said the poky little puppy.

The four little puppies listened, and

they could hear it, too. "Chocolate custard!" they cried. "Someone is spooning it into our bowls!"

And home they went as fast as they could go, over the bridge, up the road, through the meadow, and under the fence. And there, sure enough, was dinner waiting for them, with chocolate custard for dessert.

But their mother was greatly displeased. "So you're the little puppies who will dig holes under fences!" she said. "No chocolate custard tonight!" And she made them go straight to bed.

But the poky little puppy came home after everyone else was sound asleep, and he ate up all the chocolate custard and crawled into bed as happy as a lark.

The next morning someone had filled the hole and put up a sign. The sign said:

BUT. . . . .

In spite of that, the five little puppies dug a hole under the fence and went for a walk in the wide, wide world.

Through the meadow they went, down the road, over the bridge, across the green grass, and up the hill, two and two. And when they got to the top of the hill they counted themselves: one, two, three, four. One little puppy wasn't there.

"Now where in the world is that poky little puppy?" they wondered. For he certainly wasn't on top of the hill.

He wasn't going down the other side. The only thing they could see going down was a little grass snake.

He wasn't coming up this side. The only thing they could see coming up was a big grasshopper.

But when they looked down at the grassy place near the bottom of the hill,

there he was, looking hard at something on the ground in front of him.

"What is he doing?" the four little puppies asked one another. And down they went to see, roly-poly, pell-mell, tumble-bumble, till they came to the green grass; and there they stopped short.

"What in the world are you doing?" they asked.

"I see something!" said the poky little puppy.

The four little puppies looked, and they could see it, too. It was a ripe, red strawberry growing there in the grass.

"Strawberry shortcake!" they cried.

And home they went as fast as they could go, over the bridge, up the road,

through the meadow, and under the fence. And there, sure enough, was dinner waiting for them, with strawberry shortcake for dessert.

But their mother said: "So you're the little puppies who dug that hole under the fence again! No strawberry shortcake for supper tonight!" And she made them go straight to bed.

But the four little puppies waited until they thought she was asleep, and then they slipped out and filled up the hole, and when they turned around, there was their mother watching them.

"What good little puppies!" she said. "Come have some strawberry shortcake!"

And this time, when the poky little puppy got home, he had to squeeze in through a wide place in the fence. And there were his four brothers and sisters, licking the last crumbs from their saucer.

"Dear me!" said his mother. "What a pity you're so poky! Now the strawberry shortcake is all gone!"

So the poky little puppy had to go to bed without a single bite of shortcake, and he felt very sorry for himself.

And the next morning someone had put up a sign that read:

The ANIMALS *of* FARMER JONES

By LEAH GALE

Illustrated by RICHARD SCARRY

The sheep sniff around the barn.
"Ba-a-a, ba-a-a-a," say the sheep.
"We're waiting for supper."
But where is Farmer Jones?

The cat rubs against a post.
"Me-o-w, me-o-w," says the cat.
"My dish is empty."
But where is Farmer Jones?

It is supper time on the farm.
The animals are very hungry.
But where is Farmer Jones?

The horse stamps in his stall.
"I want my supper."
But where is Farmer Jones?

"Cluck, cluck," say the chickens.
"Give us our supper."
But where is Farmer Jones?

The ducks waddle out of the pond.
"Quack, quack," say the ducks.
"Supper time, supper time."
But where is Farmer Jones?

The pigs snuffle in the trough.
"Oink, oink," say the pigs.
"There's nothing to eat."
But where is Farmer Jones?

The cow jangles her bell.
"Moo, moo," says the cow.
"I am very hungry."
But where is Farmer Jones?

The dog runs about barking.
"Wuff, wuff," says the dog.
"I want my meal."
But where is Farmer Jones?

Farmer Jones is out in the field.
"Six o'clock!" says Farmer Jones.
"It's supper time!"
He goes to get food for the animals.

He gives oats to the horse.
"Nei-g-hh, nei-g-hh," says the horse.
"Thank you, Farmer Jones."

He gives turnips to the sheep.
"Ba-a-a, ba-a-a-a," say the sheep.
"Thank you, Farmer Jones."

He gives milk to the cat.
"Me-e-o-w, me-e-o-w," says the cat.
"Thank you, Farmer Jones."

He gives corn to the chickens.
"Cluck, cluck," say the chickens.
"Thank you, Farmer Jones."

He gives barley to the ducks.
"Quack, quack," say the ducks.
"Thank you, Farmer Jones."

He gives mash to the pigs.
"Oink, oink," say the pigs.
"Thank you, Farmer Jones."

He gives grain to the cow.
"Moo, moo," says the cow.
"Thank you, Farmer Jones."

He gives bones to the dog.
"Wuff, wuff," says the dog.
"Thank you, Farmer Jones."

"I am hungry, too," says Farmer Jones.
And off he goes for his supper.

TOOTLE

By GERTRUDE CRAMPTON

Illustrated by TIBOR GERGELY

Far, far to the west of everywhere is the village of Lower Trainswitch. All the baby locomotives go there to learn to be big locomotives. The young locomotives steam up and down the tracks, trying to call out the long, sad *Toooooooo* of the big locomotives. But the best they can do is a gay little *Tootle*, and the villagers smile as they listen to the young locomotives practice.

Lower Trainswitch has a fine school for engines. There are lessons in Whistle Blowing, Stopping for a Red Flag Waving, Puffing Loudly When Starting, Coming Around Curves Safely, Screeching When Stopping, Clicking and Clacking When Going Over the Rails, and Staying on the Rails No Matter What. Young locomotives must study all these lessons.

Then, too, there are other things to study. For those who wish to be freight trains there are How to Carry Milk Without Turning It to Butter, Freight Train Whistling, and Watching the Caboose. For passenger trains there are lessons in Going Through Tunnels, Pulling the Diner Without Spilling the Soup, and How Beds are Made in Trains.

Of all the things that are taught in the Lower Trainswitch School for Locomotives, the most important is, of course, Staying on the Rails No Matter What.

The head of the school is an old engineer named Bill. Bill always tells the new locomotives that he will not be angry if they sometimes spill the soup pulling the diner, or if they turn the milk to butter now and then. But they will never, never be good trains unless they get 100 A+ in Staying on the Rails No Matter What. All the baby engines work very hard to get 100 A+ in Staying on the Rails. After a few weeks not one of the engines in the Lower Trainswitch School for Trains would even think of going off the rails, no matter—well, no matter what.

One day a new locomotive named Tootle came to school.

"Here is the finest baby I've seen since old 600," thought Bill. He patted the gleaming young locomotive and said, "How would you like to grow up to be the flyer between New York and Chicago?"

"If a Flyer goes very fast, I should like to be one," Tootle answered. "I love to go fast. Watch me."

He raced all around the roundhouse.

"Good! Good!" said Bill. "You must study Whistle Blowing, Puffing Loudly When Starting, Stopping for a Red Flag Waving, Pulling the Diner Without Spilling the Soup, and all kinds of things.

"But most of all you must study Staying on the Rails No Matter What. Remember, you can't be a Flyer unless you get 100 A+ in Staying on the Rails."

Tootle promised that he would remember and that he would work very hard. All the people in Lower Trainswitch began to talk about him. They said he could pull a baby diner up hill and down again without spilling one drop of soup. And in just six lessons. They told about his high grades in Puffing, Whistle Blowing, and Clicking and Clacking. Tootle was the pet of the town.

He even worked hard at Stopping for a Red Flag Waving. Tootle did not like those lessons at all. There is nothing a locomotive hates more than stopping.

But Bill said that no locomotive ever, ever kept going when he saw a red flag waving.

"Stopping for a Red Flag Waving is almost as important as Staying on the Rails No Matter What," said Bill.

"Well, all right," Tootle grumbled. "I don't like to stop, though. I like to go fast."

"Yes, I know," said Bill. "You are like all Flyers. But you can go fast when you see the green flag."

One day, while Tootle was practicing for his lesson in Staying on the Rails No Matter What, a dreadful thing happened.

He looked across the meadow he was running through and saw a fine, strong black horse.

"Race you to the river," shouted the black horse, and kicked up his heels.

Away went the horse. His black tail

streamed out behind him, and his mane tossed in the wind. Oh, how he could run!

"Here I go," said Tootle to himself.

"If I am going to be a Flyer, I can't let a horse beat me," he puffed. "Everyone at school will laugh at me."

His wheels turned so fast that they were silver streaks. The cars lurched and bumped together. And just as Tootle was sure he could win, the tracks made a great curve.

"Oh, Whistle!" cried Tootle. "That horse will beat me now. He'll run straight while I take the Great Curve."

Then the Dreadful Thing happened. After all that Bill had said about Staying on the Rails No Matter What, Tootle jumped off the tracks and raced alongside the black horse!

The race ended in a tie. Both Tootle and the black horse were happy. Tootle was pleased because the horse hadn't won, and the horse was happy because he had never before been so close to beating a locomotive. They stood on the bank of the river and talked.

"It's nice out here in the meadow," Tootle said.

"Yes, but I thought you fellows had to stay on the rails," said the horse in a puzzled way.

"We do, but I didn't," Tootle explained.

"Oh," said the horse.

When Tootle got back to school, he said nothing about leaving the rails. But he thought about it that night in the roundhouse.

"Tomorrow I will work hard," decided Tootle. "I will not even think of leaving the rails, no matter what."

And he did work hard. He practiced tootling so much that the Mayor Himself ran up the hill, his green coattails flapping, and said that everyone in the village had a headache and would he please stop TOOTLING.

So Tootle was sent to practice Staying on the Rails No Matter What.

As he came to the Great Curve, Tootle looked across the meadow. It was full of buttercups.

"It's like a big yellow carpet. How I should like to play in them and hold one under my searchlight to see if I like butter!" thought Tootle. "But no, I am going to be a Flyer and I must practice Staying on the Rails No Matter What!"

Tootle clicked and clacked around the Great Curve. His wheels began to say over and over again, "Do you like butter? Do you?"

"I don't know," said Tootle crossly. "But I'm going to find out."

He stopped much faster than any good Flyer ever does, unless he is stopping for a Red Flag Waving. The sparks shot from his wheels and the eight bowls of soup rolled around and around. He hopped off the tracks and bumped along the meadow to the yellow buttercups.

"I do like butter!" cried Tootle. "I do!"

At last the sun began to go down, and it was time to hurry to the roundhouse.

That evening while the Chief Oiler was playing checkers with old Bill, he said, "It's queer. It's very queer, but I found grass between Tootle's front wheels today."

"Hmm," said Bill. "There must be grass growing on the tracks."

"Not on our tracks," said the Day Watchman, who spent his days watching the tracks and his nights watching Bill and the Chief Oiler play checkers.

Bill's face was stern. "Tootle knows he must get 100 A+ in Staying on the Rails No Matter What, if he's going to be a Flyer."

Next day Tootle played all day in the meadow. He watched a green frog and he made a daisy chain. He found a rain

"What fun!" said Tootle.

And he danced around and around and held one of the buttercups under his searchlight. Then he ran to the river and peeked into the quiet water to see if he liked butter.

barrel, and he said softly, "Toot!"

"TOOT!" shouted the barrel.

"Why, I sound like a Flyer already!" cried Tootle.

That night the First Assistant Oiler said he had found a daisy in Tootle's bell. The day after that, the Second Assistant Oiler said that he had found hollyhock flowers floating in Tootle's eight bowls of soup.

And then the Mayor Himself said that he had seen Tootle chasing butterflies in the meadow. The Mayor Himself said that Tootle had looked very silly, too.

Early one morning Bill had a long, long talk with the Mayor Himself.

When the Mayor Himself left the Lower Trainswitch School for Locomotives, he laughed all the way to the village.

"Bill's plan will surely put Tootle back on the track," he chuckled.

Bill ran from one store to the next, buying ten yards of this and twenty yards of that and all you have of the other. The Chief Oiler and the First, Second, and Third Assistant Oilers were hammering and sawing instead of oiling and polishing. And Tootle? Well, Tootle was in the meadow watching the butterflies flying and wishing he could dip and soar as they did.

That afternoon everyone in Lower Trainswitch crowded into the office of the Mayor Himself. "Yes, yes!" they shouted when the Mayor Himself asked if they wanted to help Tootle. Then the Mayor Himself said, "Bill has a plan. If you do just as he says, I think we can teach young Tootle how to be a Flyer."

After that, Bill stood up and said things like this: "Now, you know that all locomotives. . . . Of course, every locomotive. . . . As I say, the thing is. . . . And if you will. . . ."

Then all the people laughed and promised to help. When they went home, each had a piece of ten yards of this and the twenty yards of that nailed to one of the sticks the Oilers had hammered and sawed all morning.

Not a store in Lower Trainswitch was open the next day and not a person was at home. By the time the sun came up, every villager was hiding in the meadow along the tracks. And each of them had a red flag. It had taken all the

red goods in Lower Trainswitch, and hard work by the Oilers, but there was a red flag for everyone.

Soon Tootle came tootling happily down the tracks.

"Today I shall watch the bluebirds very carefully. Perhaps I can find out how they fly," he said to himself, and played a gay little song on his whistle.

When he came to the meadow, he hopped off the tracks and rolled along the grass. Just as he was thinking what a beautiful day it was, a red flag poked up from the grass and waved hard. Tootle stopped, for every locomotive knows he must stop for a Red Flag Waving.

"I'll go another way," said Tootle.

He turned to the left and up came another waving red flag, this time from the middle of the buttercups.

"Oh, Whistle!" said Tootle and stamped his cowcatcher hard. "Very well, I will go to the right and play toot-TOOT with the rain barrel."

When he went to the right, there was another red flag.

There were red flags waving from the buttercups, in the daisies, under the trees, near the bluebirds' nest, and even one behind the rain barrel. And, of course, Tootle had to stop for each one, for a locomotive must always Stop for a Red Flag Waving.

"Red flags," muttered Tootle. "This meadow is full of red flags. How can I have any fun?

"Whenever I start, I have to stop. Why did I think this meadow was such a fine place? Why don't I ever see a green flag?"

Just as the tears were ready to slide out of his boiler, Tootle happened to look back over his coal car. On the tracks stood Bill, and in his hand was a big green flag. "Oh!" said Tootle.

He puffed up to Bill and stopped.

"This is the place for me," said Tootle. "There are nothing but red flags for locomotives that get off their tracks."

"Hurray!" shouted the people of Lower Trainswitch, and jumped up from their hiding places. "Hurray for Tootle the Flyer!"

Now Tootle is a famous Two-Miles-a-Minute Flyer. The young locomotives listen to his advice.

"Work hard," he tells them. "Always remember to stop for a Red Flag Waving. But most of all, Stay on the Rails No Matter What."

THE NEW HOUSE IN THE FOREST

By LUCY SPRAGUE MITCHELL

Illustrated by ELOISE WILKIN

The Jenks family wanted to build a new house.

The question was, where should they build it?

Mr. Jenks, the father of the family, wanted the house to be near the town where he worked. Mrs. Jenks, the mother of the family, wanted the house to be where it could have running water and electricity.

Timmy and Judy Jenks—they were the children of the family—wanted the house to be where many animals lived.

"I know just the spot," said Mr. Jenks. "Let's jump into our little old auto and drive out to see what you think of it."

So Mr. and Mrs. Jenks and Timmy and Judy jumped into their little old auto. Off they drove to a big forest with a river winding through it.

"This is near the town where I work," said Mr. Jenks.

"Our house could have running water and electricity here," said Mrs. Jenks.

"I bet bears and squirrels and owls and all sorts of animals live in this forest," said Timmy and Judy.

The Jenks family liked the forest with the river.

They all said, "We'll make a new home here."

The animals in the forest heard them.

"Chee, chee, chee!" chattered a mother squirrel high in a tree. "They might like to live in a hole in a tree, like me. There's an empty hole near mine."

"Grrrrr!" growled a big brown bear. "The Jenks family might like to live in a cave like me. There's an empty cave near mine."

"To-whoo! To-whoo!" called a big gray owl. "All this noise has woken me up. The Jenks family can have a hole in my tree if they will sleep all day. Goodbye! I'm going to sleep again!"

In the river swam the silvery fish. They opened their round fish mouths and bubbles bubbled out. They said, "We like our water home in the forest. The Jenks family might move in here with us."

Timmy and Judy laughed, for they understood what the fish and the animals were saying. "You just wait and see the house we are going to build!" they called back.

"We will have to have many workers to help us build our new house," said Mr. Jenks.

So the next day Mr. Jenks went off to the town and found three men to help him chop down the trees. "We must make an open place for the new house," said Mr. Jenks.

Soon all the animals in the forest heard the men chop, chop, chopping.

"Chee, chee, chee!" scolded the mother squirrel. "Don't chop down my tree! Can't you see I have a family in this tree?"

"To-whoo, to-whoo!" said the owl.

"You woke me up again. Don't chop down my tree."

"Grrrrr!" growled the brown bear. "Don't chop down the tree where the wild bees keep their honey. I like to eat honey."

Timmy and Judy understood what the animals said. So they asked their father and the men not to chop down the squirrel's tree or the owl's tree or the bear's honey tree.

The men chopped down many trees but they left those trees for the animals. They chopped off the branches of the fallen trees. Now the fallen trees were logs.

Then Mr. Jenks and the three men brought some strong horses. The strong horses dragged the logs to the river. The men threw the logs into the river with a big splash.

"Don't fill up our river with logs," bubbled the silvery fish. "The river is our home."

"The logs won't spoil your river, little fish," said Timmy.

"Your river will carry the logs down to the sawmill to be made into lumber for our new house. You can go on living in the river, little fish," said Judy.

The sawmill sawed the logs into lumber. It sawed big strong pieces, flat boards, and shingles. The lumber had to stand in piles for a while to be seasoned.

Then a big truck brought the lumber back to the clearing in the forest. The men piled up the big strong pieces, the flat boards, and the shingles for the new house.

"Before we build the house, we must dig a cellar," said Mr. Jenks.

So the men helped Mr. Jenks dig a hole just the size the new house was to be. They rolled big stones from the forest into the hole. Then they built the cellar walls out of the stones.

The big brown bear looked down into the cellar. "Grrrrr!" growled the bear. "Is the Jenks family going to live in a hole?"

Timmy and Judy laughed, for they knew what the cellar was for and the bear didn't.

Next Mr. Jenks got two carpenters to help him build the new house. All the animals heard the bang, bang, banging as the carpenters pounded nails into the lumber. The carpenters nailed the strong pieces of lumber together and made a frame for the house.

Then the carpenters nailed flat boards to the frame to make the floors and walls. They sawed up some boards to build the stairs to the attic. Then they nailed more boards to the frame for the roof. And over the roof they nailed shingles.

"Chee, chee, chee," said the mother squirrel to her babies. "Come and see what a queer thing these men are building out of the trees."

Timmy and Judy laughed because the squirrels had never seen a house before and didn't know what it was.

Of course the Jenks family wanted to have a fireplace for popping corn at Halloween and for hanging their stockings at Christmas. And they needed a chimney for the smoke from the fireplace. So they got the chimney mason to come to build it.

First he had to make the footing for the chimney to rest on. Next he made a brick hearth. Then he was ready for the fire brick to line the fireplace. That was the hard part—to make it so that it would not smoke. Last of all he used hollow tiles for the inside of the chimney and put stone on the outside from the ground to the top of the roof.

Then Mr. Jenks got two plumbers to help him bring the water from the river to the new house. The plumbers dug a ditch from the house to a place where the river was higher than the house. In the ditch they laid pipes. They ran the pipes into the cellar. They cut holes in the ceiling of the cellar and ran the pipes up the walls inside the house. They ran some pipes to the kitchen and other pipes to the bathroom.

The silvery fish saw the plumbers put the end of the pipe into their river. When the plumbers turned on the water in the kitchen, the fish heard the water in the river gurgle as it ran into the pipe.

"Don't take the water from our river!" said the fish, sending up many bubbles.

"Little fish," said Judy, "we need water in our new house to wash in and to cook with. But there will be plenty of water left in the river for you."

Then Mr. Jenks got the furnace men. The furnace men put a big furnace in the cellar. The furnace men ran big pipes from the furnace along the ceiling of the cellar. They cut holes in the ceiling right up into the rooms above. They fitted registers into the holes in the floors of the rooms above. Then they built a fire in the furnace. The heat went through the big pipes to the rooms above.

Then Mr. Jenks had the electricians come. The electricians strung a long wire from the electricity poles on the road to the house. They ran the wire into the cellar of the house. Then they ran wires up the walls to every room in the house. At the ends of the wires they screwed electric bulbs so every room could be light at night.

Then Mr. Jenks got the plasterers to come and put plaster on the walls inside the house. The plasterers shook the white plaster out of bags and mixed it with water.

Then the painters painted the outside of the house. They painted the plaster walls inside the house. They painted the attic room a jolly green.

"Chee, chee, chee," said the mother squirrel, sitting on the window sill looking in. "This room looks just like the trees. I like it."

"We like it, too," said Timmy and Judy. "It is our room."

Now the new house in the forest was ready for the Jenks family. So the next day they moved.

The moving van brought furniture, china, pots, and pans, and a big box full of Timmy's and Judy's toys. Timmy and Judy helped put things in place.

Now the Jenks family was really at home in their new house in the forest.

Every afternoon after that, as soon as he was through working in town, Mr. Jenks jumped into his little auto and drove out to the new house.

If it was dark when he came home, the lights were on inside and the house was bright.

"Hello, new house!" said Mr. Jenks. "I like to see you all light and bright."

"Grrrr!" growled the bear, peering out of his dark cave in the forest. "The Jenks family is queer to like light in their rooms."

Every day after that Mrs. Jenks cooked dinner in the new kitchen. She turned on the faucet and water from the river ran out. She turned on the stove and the electric wires in the stove got hot.

"I'm happy as a cricket in our new house in the forest with running water and electricity," said Mrs. Jenks.

"Chreep!" chirped a happy cricket from a warm corner of the kitchen. "I like it here, too."

Every evening after that Timmy and Judy had supper in the kitchen.

"I'm glad our new house is in a forest where bees live," said Timmy, as he spread wild honey on his bread and handed the jar of honey to Judy.

"Buzz-zz-zz," said a little honey bee. "These children seem to like my honey. Tomorrow I'll have to buzz off and find some flowers and make some more."

Every night after that Judy and Timmy went to bed in their attic room. In the dark of night the big white owl flew like a white shadow through the forest. He could see in the dark. He looked in at the window and saw Judy and Timmy in their beds.

"To-whoo," he called. "These are queer children to sleep at night. That's when I'm awake."

But Timmy and Judy did not hear the owl. They were sound asleep in their new house in the forest.

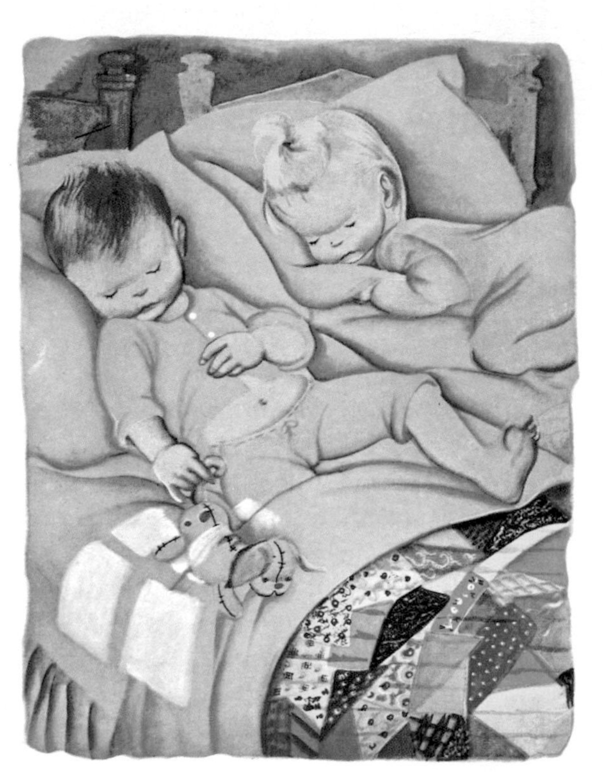

The Taxi That Hurried

By LUCY SPRAGUE MITCHELL,
IRMA SIMONTON BLACK,
and JESSIE STANTON

Illustrated by TIBOR GERGELY

Once there was a taxi. It was a bright yellow with two red lines running around its body. Inside it had a soft leather seat and two hard little let-down seats.

It was a smart little taxi. For it could start fast—jerk-whizz!! It could tear along the street—whizz-squeak!! It could stop fast—squeak-jerk!!

Its driver's name was Bill. Together they were a speedy pair.

One day the taxi was standing on the street close to the sidewalk. Bill and the little taxi didn't like to stand still long. "I wonder who will be our next passengers," thought Bill.

Just then Bill heard some feet running on the sidewalk, thump, thump, thump! And he heard some smaller feet pattering along, too, thumpety, thumpety, thumpety!

He leaned out and saw Tom with a little suitcase and Tom's mother with a big suitcase. And both of them were breathing hard.

"Oh!" gasped Tom's mother. "Taxi driver-man, please drive us to the station as fast as you can. We're very late and the train won't wait. Oh!—oh!—oh!"

Tom and his mother tumbled into the taxi and slammed the door.

"Sure, lady," answered Bill. "We're a speedy pair. We can get you there."

Away went the taxi.

It liked to tear along in a hurry, purring softly. It rushed down the street like a yellow streak with the two red lines blurred into one around its middle. It wiggled through the traffic.

Tom and his mother bounced and jounced on the leather seats. Tom's mother sat on the wide, soft one behind. But Tom sat on a hard little one so that he could look out of the window.

Then suddenly, squeak-jerk! The taxi stopped short. It stood stock still in the middle of the street. Ahead shone a bright red light. Underneath the light stood a big traffic policeman holding up his right hand.

Tom's mother called through the window, "Taxi driver-man, must you stop when lights are red? We simply have to get ahead. We're *terribly* late and the train won't wait."

And Bill answered, "Surely, lady, you have seen how cars must wait until the lights are green. But we're a speedy pair, we'll surely get you there." Then suddenly, jerk-whizz! They were off again down the crowded street.

For the light had changed to green again.

Away went the taxi down the street faster than ever. Now it had to turn and twist, for the street was full of traffic—trucks and wagons and other taxis. The little taxi hurried past them all like a yellow streak and people could hardly see Tom's little face looking out of the window as he bounced and jounced by.

"My!" said the people on the sidewalk. "That's a speedy taxi. I wonder why it's in such a hurry. Lucky it's got such a good driver." The taxi wiggled around a big bus. It jiggled across a trolley track. Then suddenly, squeak-jerk! The little taxi stopped short again.

It stood stock still behind a big coal truck that was backing up to the sidewalk. For the driver was trying hard to get his truck just the right way for the black coal to go jumping and clattering down its slide into a hole in the sidewalk.

Tom stood up so that he could see the big coal truck better. He could see the handle on the side. He wished he could watch the driver turn that handle and make the big truck tip up in front. He almost wished they weren't in a hurry.

Tom's mother called through the open window: "Taxi driver-man, first it's a cop that makes you stop and now we're stuck behind a truck. We're *awfully* late and the train won't wait."

So Bill called to the truck driver, "Please, will you try to let me get by?"

And the truck driver grinned and stopped his truck. Carefully and slowly Bill squeezed by the big coal truck, close to the sidewalk.

Bill called over his shoulder, "We're a speedy pair. We'll get you there."

Now the taxi went so fast that people skipped up onto the sidewalk as it went by and everyone thought: "That's the speediest taxi I ever saw!" Then suddenly, squeak-jerk! The taxi stopped short and Tom almost fell through the front window.

Tom's mother bounced so hard on the wide leather seat that her head whacked the ceiling of the taxi. Her hat slid down over one ear. Her big suitcase fell over with a bang on the floor and Tom's little suitcase hopped off the seat.

Tom's mother pulled her hat on straight again. Then she looked at her watch. Then she looked out of the window at all the taxis and buses and trucks.

Once more she called to Bill on the front seat: "Taxi driver-man, first it's a cop that makes you stop; then you get stuck behind a truck. Now the traffic is in our way. We're likely to sit here the rest of the day. We're *horribly* late and the train won't wait!"

So Bill began to blow his horn. "Honk! honk!" shrieked the little taxi. "Honk! honk! HONK!!

"We want to go. You make us slow! We're a speedy pair. We want to get there. Honk! *Honk!*"

HONK!!! HONK!!!

The nearer they came to the station, the more taxis and buses and trucks there were on the street.

Suddenly they stopped, and Bill blew the horn again. "Honk! *Honk!* HONK!"

Down the street, up above the station, they could see the big station clock. In five minutes the train would go. They really were very, terribly, awfully, horribly late, and they knew the train wouldn't wait.

Then suddenly, jerk, jerk! The traffic began to move. First a taxi, then a bus, then a truck, then more taxis, more buses, more trucks, till the whole line was moving. The speedy little taxi wiggled through the traffic. It dodged around a bus and it twisted around a truck and it whizzed past a taxi. Tom's mother kept looking at the big station clock. It said four minutes before the train went. Then three minutes. Then two minutes—and the little taxi drew up by the station.

Tom jumped out of the taxi while his mother gave Bill the money. She grabbed her big suitcase. Tom grabbed his little suitcase. And off they ran, thump, thump, thump, thumpety, thumpety, thumpety.

Bill looked after them and grinned at his yellow taxi. "Sure," he said. "We're a speedy pair—we got them there."

And it was true. The conductor was just ready to signal the engineer to start.

But he saw Tom and his mother come running down the platform and he waited for them. He took the big suitcase from Tom's mother, held the door open for her, and handed her the big suitcase. Tom stepped on the train after her, panting from his run and holding his little suitcase.

"All aboard!" called the conductor, waving his hand to the engineer.

Then the conductor swung onto the train just as it began to move. "You're a fast runner," he said to Tom. And to Tom's mother he said, "Lady, you just made it."

Tom was still breathing hard but he managed to gasp out, "We made it—because—we had such a speedy taxi—and speedy driver. You should have seen—that taxi hurry!"

SCUFFY THE TUGBOAT

and His Adventures Down the River

By GERTRUDE CRAMPTON

Illustrated by
TIBOR GERGELY

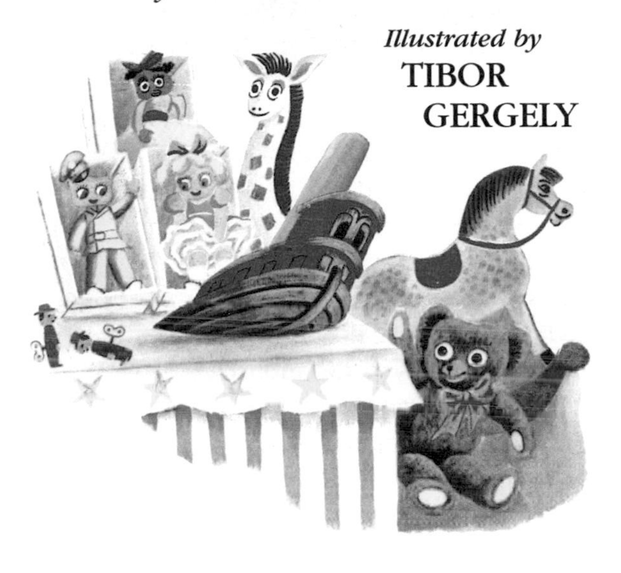

Scuffy was sad. Scuffy was cross. Scuffy sniffed his blue smokestack.

"A toy store is no place for a red-painted tugboat," said Scuffy, and he sniffed his blue smokestack again. "I was meant for bigger things."

"Perhaps you would not be cross if you went sailing," said the man with the polka dot tie, who owned the shop.

So one night he took Scuffy home to his little boy. He filled the bathtub with water.

"Sail, little tugboat," said the little boy.

"I won't sail in a bathtub," said Scuffy. "A tub is no place for a red-painted tugboat. I was meant for bigger things."

The next day the man with the polka dot tie and his little boy carried Scuffy to a laughing brook that started high in the hills.

"Sail, little tugboat," said the man with the polka dot tie.

It was Spring, and the brook was full to the brim with its water. And the water moved in a hurry, as all things move in a hurry when it is Spring.

Scuffy was in a hurry, too.

"Come back little tugboat, come back," cried the little boy as the hurrying, brimful brook carried Scuffy downstream.

"Not I," tooted Scuffy. "Not I. This is the life for me."

All that day Scuffy sailed along with the brook.

Past the meadows filled with cowslips. Past the women washing clothes on the bank. Past the little woods filled with violets.

Cows came to the brook to drink.

They stood in the cool water, and it was fun to sail around between their legs and bump softly into their noses.

It was fun to see them drink.

But when a white and brown cow almost drank Scuffy instead of the brook's cool water, Scuffy was frightened. That was not fun!

Night came, and with it the moon.

There was nothing to see but the quiet trees.

Suddenly an owl called out, "Hoot, hooot!"

"Toot, tooot!" cried the frightened tugboat, and he wished he could see the smiling, friendly face of the man with the polka dot tie.

When morning came, Scuffy was cross instead of frightened.

"I was meant for bigger things, but which way am I to go?" he said. But there was only one way to go, and that was with the running water where the two brooks met to form a small river. And with the river sailed Scuffy, the red-painted tugboat.

He was proud when he sailed past villages.

"People build villages at the edge of my river," said Scuffy, and he straightened his blue smokestack.

Once Scuffy's river joined a small one jammed with logs. Here were men in heavy jackets and great boots, walking about on the floating logs, trying to pry them free.

"Toot, toot, let me through," demanded Scuffy. But the men paid no attention to him. They pushed the logs apart so they would drift with the river to the sawmill in the town.

Scuffy bumped along with the jostling logs.

"Ouch!" he cried as two logs bumped together.

"This is a fine river," said Scuffy, "but it's very busy and very big for me."

He was proud when he sailed under the bridges.

"My river is so wide and so deep that people must build bridges to cross it."

The river moved through big towns now instead of villages.

And the bridges over it were very wide—wide enough so that many cars and trucks and streetcars could cross all at once.

The river got deeper and deeper. Scuffy did not have to tuck up his bottom.

The river moved faster and faster.

"I feel like a train instead of a tugboat," said Scuffy, as he was hurried along.

He was proud when he passed the old sawmill with its water wheel.

But high in the hills and mountains the winter snow melted. Water filled the brooks and rushed from there into the small rivers. Faster and faster it flowed, to the great river where Scuffy sailed.

"There is too much water in this river," said Scuffy, as he pitched and tossed on the waves. "Soon it will splash over the top and what a flood there will be!"

Soon great armies of men came to save the fields and towns from the rushing water.

On went the river to the sea. At last Scuffy sailed into a big city. Here the river widened, and all about were docks and wharves.

Oh, it was a busy place and a noisy place! The cranes groaned as they swung the cargoes into great ships. The porters shouted as they carried suitcases and boxes on board.

They filled bags with sand and put them at the edge of the river.

"They're making higher banks for the river," shouted Scuffy, "to hold the water back." The water rose higher and higher.

The men built the sand bags higher and higher. Higher! went the river. Higher! went the sand bags.

At last the water rose no more. The flood water rushed on to the sea, and Scuffy raced along with the flood. The people and the fields and the towns were safe.

Horses stamped and truck motors roared, streetcars clanged and people shouted. Scuffy said, "Toot, toot," but nobody noticed.

"Oh, oh!" cried Scuffy when he saw the sea. "There is no beginning and no end to the sea. I wish I could find the man with the polka dot tie and his little boy!"

Just as the little red-painted tugboat sailed past the last piece of land, a hand reached out and picked him up. And there was the man with the polka dot tie, with his little boy beside him.

Scuffy is home now with the man with the polka dot tie and his little boy.

He sails from one end of the bathtub to the other.

"This is the place for a red-painted tugboat," says Scuffy. "And this is the life for me."

THE SAGGY BAGGY ELEPHANT

By KATHRYN *and* BYRON JACKSON

Illustrated by GUSTAF TENGGREN

A happy little elephant was dancing through the jungle. He thought he was dancing beautifully, one-two-three-kick. But whenever he went one-two-three, his big feet pounded so that they shook the whole jungle. And whenever he went kick, he kicked over a tree or a bush.

The little elephant danced along leaving wreckage behind him, until one day, he met a parrot.

"Why are you shaking the jungle all to pieces?" cried the parrot, who had never before seen an elephant. "What kind of animal are you, anyway?"

The little elephant said, "I don't know what kind of animal I am. I live all alone in the jungle. I dance and I kick—and I call myself Sooki. It's a good-sounding name, and it fits me, don't you think?"

"Maybe," answered the parrot, "but if it does it's the only thing that *does* fit you. Your ears are too big for you, and your nose is way too big for you. And your skin is *much*, MUCH too big for you. It's baggy and saggy. You should call yourself Saggy-Baggy!"

Sooki sighed. His pants *did* look pretty wrinkled.

"I'd be glad to improve myself," he said, "but I don't know how to go about it. What shall I do?"

"I can't tell you. I never saw anything like you in all my life!" replied the parrot.

The little elephant tried to smooth out his skin. He rubbed it with his trunk. That did no good.

He pulled up his pants legs—but they fell right back into dozens of wrinkles.

It was very disappointing, and the parrot's saucy laugh didn't help a bit.

Just then a tiger came walking along. He was a beautiful, sleek tiger. His skin fit him like a glove.

Sooki rushed up to him and said:

"Tiger, please tell me why your skin fits so well! The parrot says mine is all baggy and saggy, and I do want to make it fit me like yours fits you!"

The tiger didn't care a foot about Sooki's troubles, but he did feel flattered and important, and he did feel just a mite hungry.

"My skin always did fit," said the tiger. "Maybe it's because I take a lot of exercise. But . . ." added the tiger, ". . . if you don't care for exercise, I shall be delighted to nibble a few of those extra pounds of skin off for you!"

"Oh no, thank you! No, thank you!" cried Sooki. "I love exercise! Just watch me!"

Sooki ran until he was well beyond reach.

Then he did somersaults and rolled on his back. He walked on his hind legs and he walked on his front legs.

When Sooki wandered down to the river to get a big drink of water, he met the parrot. The parrot laughed harder than ever.

"I tried exercising," sighed the little elephant. "Now I don't know what to do."

"Soak in the water the way the crocodile does," laughed the parrot. "Maybe your skin will shrink."

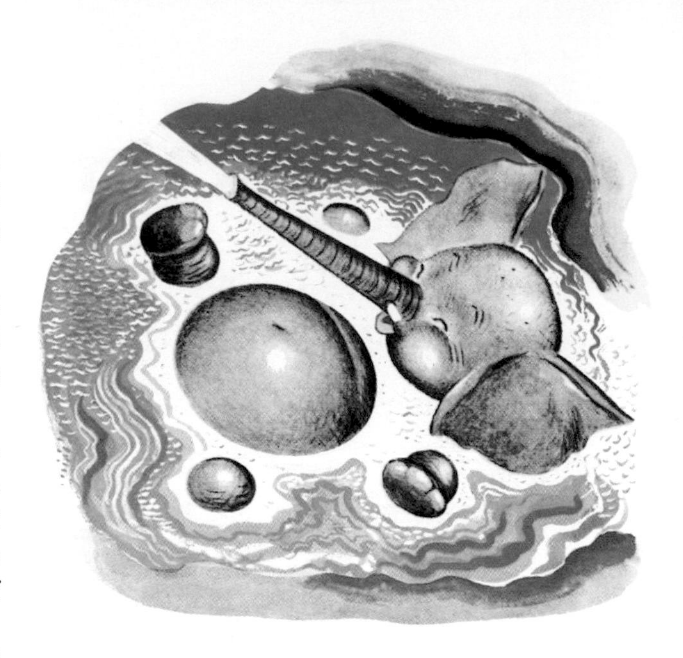

So Sooki tramped straight into the water.

But before he had soaked nearly long enough to shrink his skin, a great big crocodile came swimming up, snapping his fierce jaws and looking greedily at Sooki's tender ears.

The little elephant clambered up the bank and ran away, feeling very discouraged.

"I'd better hide in a dark place where my bags and sags and creases and wrinkles won't show," he said.

By and by he found a deep dark cave, and with a heavy sigh he tramped inside and sat down.

Suddenly, he heard a fierce growling and grumbling and snarling. He peeped out of the cave and saw a lion padding down the path.

"I'm hungry!" roared the lion. "I haven't had a thing to eat today. Not a thing except a thin, bony antelope, and a puny monkey—and a buffalo, but such a tough one! And two turtles, but you can't count turtles. There's nothing much to eat between those saucers they wear for clothes! I'm *hungry!* I could eat an *elephant!*"

And he began to pad straight toward the dark cave where the little elephant was hidden.

"This is the end of me, sags, bags, wrinkles and creases," thought Sooki, and he let out one last, trumpeting bellow!

Just as he did, the jungle was filled with a terrible crashing and an awful stomping. A whole herd of great gray wrinkled elephants came charging up, and the big hungry lion jumped up in the air, turned around, and ran away as fast as he could go.

Sooki peered out of the cave and all the big elephants smiled at him. Sooki thought they were the most beautiful creatures he had ever seen. "I wish I looked just like you," he said.

"You do," grinned the big elephants. "You're a perfectly dandy little elephant!"

And that made Sooki so happy that he began to dance one-two-three kick through the jungle, with all those big, brave, friendly elephants behind him. The saucy parrot watched them dance. But this time he didn't laugh, not even to himself.

FIX IT, PLEASE!

By LUCY SPRAGUE MITCHELL

Illustrated by ELOISE WILKIN

Polly was a little girl. And Jimmy was a little boy, but not quite as little as Polly.

Polly and Jimmy had the same mother. And Polly and Jimmy had the same daddy. They were brother and sister.

One day Polly fell down. And her button popped right off her overalls. Polly picked up the button and ran fast, fast to Mother.

"Fix it, Mommy, please," said Polly.

So her mother sewed the button on tight.

"It's all fixed," smiled Polly. "Thank you."

One day Jimmy and Polly were eating their lunch. Jimmy jumped up in a hurry and bang! His plate fell right on the floor and broke in two.

Jimmy picked up the two pieces of the plate.

"Mommy, Mommy!" he called. "Fix my plate—it's broken. Please fix it."

"Bring me the bottle of glue, Jimmy," called his mother.

Mother took a little brush and swished the sticky glue on the edge of one piece of the broken plate. And she swished the sticky glue on the edge of the other piece. Then she pushed the two pieces together tight and put the plate away for the glue to dry.

The next day Jimmy looked at his plate. "It has a little line down the middle of it like a crack," said Jimmy. "But anyway, it's fixed. Thank you, Mother."

Pat, pat, pat ran Polly's feet, and rattle, rattle, rattled the wagon Polly was pulling. Then whang! the wagon ran into the fence and off rolled a wheel. Polly began to cry, for she was a very little girl. Then she stopped crying and ran to find her Daddy.

"My wagon broke," she said. "Fix it, please, Daddy."

So Daddy got a nut and some pliers. He put a part of the wagon through the hole in the wheel and turned and turned the nut till the wheel was tight on the wagon again.

"It's all fixed," said Polly. "It runs again."

One day Jimmy knocked his chair over. The chair fell with a crash and one of the legs broke.

"Daddy!" yelled Jimmy. "My chair is broken. Please try to fix it."

So Daddy got his tools—a saw, a hammer and some nails. He took a new piece of wood and sawed it just the right size for a new leg for the chair. Then he nailed the new leg on the chair—bang, bang!

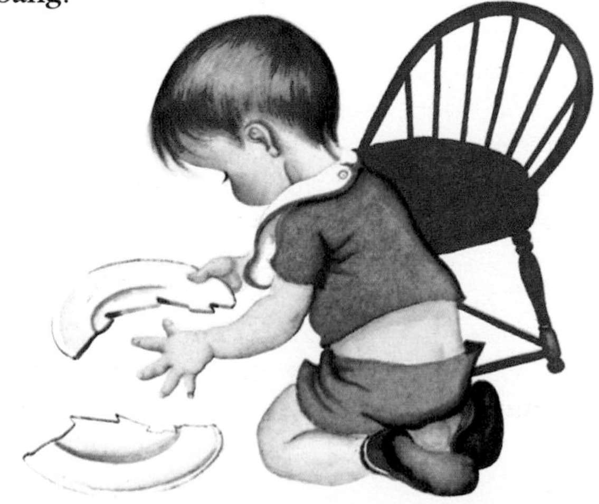

Jimmy sat down in the chair.

"It's all fixed," he said. "I can sit on it."

Polly had a rag doll named Dear-Anne. One day Dear-Anne's arm came right off.

"Dear-Anne has lost her arm," wailed Polly.

So Mother brought her needle and thread. She sewed Dear-Anne's arm on again.

"Dear-Anne is all fixed," said Polly.

And she gave Dear-Anne a big kiss.

Jimmy's play suit had no buttons. It had a zipper. Jimmy could pull the zipper up—zzzzzip! One day the zipper stuck. It wouldn't pull up.

He ran to Mother calling, "My zipper's broken."

"Zippers are hard to fix, Jimmy," said Mother.

She took her scissors and she fussed and fussed with the zipper.

"Now try it, Jimmy," she said.

Z,z,zzzzzip! It pulled up.

"It's fixed!" cried Jimmy.

One day Jimmy called, "You can't catch me!"

Polly ran fast, fast after Jimmy. Jimmy ran fast, fast away from Polly. He ran so fast he fell flat. He hurt his knee. His knee began to bleed. Jimmy began to cry. Polly began to cry too, for she was a very little girl.

Their mother came running very fast. She saw Jimmy's knee. First she kissed him. Then she said, "We'll fix your knee, Jimmy."

First she washed Jimmy's knee until there was no dirt left. Then she painted iodine on his knee. The knee looked bright yellow. Then she put a bandage on his knee and fastened the bandage with some sticky tape.

Little Polly watched it all.

"I want a bandage, too," she said.

So Mother cut off a little piece of sticky tape and put it on Polly's knee.

"Now you're both fixed up," said Mother.

One day Polly and Jimmy and Daddy and Mother got into their old car. Burrrr, the car began to shake. Then off they went, whizzing down the road.

All of a sudden, the car began to bump. It bumped and bumped though there weren't any bumps in the road.

"We've got a flat tire," said Daddy, and he sounded very mad.

"We'll get out while you fix it," said Mother.

So Daddy got out the jack and put it under the car. He moved the jack up and down until the back wheels were off the ground. Then he took the flat tire off. He took the spare tire out of the back of the car and put it on. Then he took the jack out from under the car. His hands were dirty, his trousers were dirty, his face was dirty.

"I hate to change a tire," he said.

One day Jimmy felt sick. Then Polly felt sick. Mother put them both to bed. Then she went to the telephone and called the doctor.

"Doctor," she said, "Jimmy and Polly are sick. Will you come to see them?"

The doctor came. He had a little black bag.

"Open your mouth and say 'Ah,'" said the doctor.

He looked at Jimmy's tongue and took his temperature. He looked at Polly's tongue and took her temperature. Then he opened his little black bag and took out some pink medicine.

"Here, Jimmy," said the doctor. "This pink medicine will fix you up in no time."

Jimmy swallowed the pink medicine.

The doctor was right. The next day Jimmy and Polly felt as frisky as two little puppies.

"Do you know what I am going to be when I am big?" said Jimmy to Polly.

"What?" said Polly.

"The fix-it man," said Jimmy.

"And I'll be the fix-it mommy," said Polly.

NOISES AND MR. FLIBBERTY-JIB

By
GERTRUDE CRAMPTON

Illustrated by
ELOISE WILKIN

Mr. Flibberty-jib had a most unusual rumble in his head. It went **rumble-rumble-rumble**, and then it went **bumble-bumble-bumble**.

Now, Mrs. Flibberty-jib didn't mean to, but she made Mr. Flibberty-jib's rumble and bumble worse than ever.

You see, Mrs. Flibberty-jib cooks the very finest roast beef in town. But no one can cook roast beef without closing the oven door ***ker-shut*** and covering the roasting pans ***ker-bang***.

Besides, Mrs. Flibberty-jib knits mittens all day long. And no one can knit even one mitten unless the needles say, **"Click, click, clickety click!** Click and knit! Knit and click!"

Mrs. Flibberty-jib says that Mr. Flibberty-jib has a rumble in his head because he eats too little roast beef and doesn't wear his mittens.

He says he has a large rumble in his head because the house and town are full of noises.

She says, "Nonsense!"

Then the old clock strikes, "***Bong, bong, bong!*** Three o'clock, Mr. Flibberty-jib."

The telephone shouts, "***Brr-ring! Brr-ring!*** Answer me. Quick, answer me!"

The grocery boy at the back door says, **"TAP, TAP, TAP!** Answer *me!*"

And then the telephone rings again.

"Too much noise," says Mr. Flibberty-jib.

The gray mouse that lives in the kitchen wall peeks out of the mouse hole.

"Cheese!" says the gray mouse to herself, and scampers softly over the floor like a gray shadow.

But Mrs. Flibberty-jib sees her.

"Eeeeee!" screams Mrs. Flibberty-jib.

"Squee!" squeaks little gray mouse.

"See?" says Mr. Flibberty-jib. "Too much noise."

"Nonsense!" says Mrs. Flibberty-jib, and gets off the chair.

Well, says Mr. Flibberty-jib, suppose he goes downtown to buy some red yarn for Mrs. Flibberty-jib's mittens.

The first thing he hears is —

CLANG! CLANG! CLANG!

Then, says Mr. Flibberty-jib, he walks to the curb and gets ready to cross the street. He looks to the left and right. Then he puts his left foot down. And around the corner comes—

Beep! Beep! Beep!

Then, says Mr. Flibberty-jib, he walks to the curb and gets ready to cross the street again. He looks to the left and right. Then he puts his right foot down.

And around the corner comes—

CLOP, CLOP, CLOPPETY, CLOP!

"It is no wonder," says Mr. Fliberty-jib, "that my head rumbles.

"Every time—not just once-in-a-time—I go to buy red yarn, the policeman blows his whistle,

Whee-ee-ee-ee-ee!

"The fire engine races by me, OO-oo-ooo-OO-oo-oo-oo-OO-oo-OO!

"And when I get home again, the front door always, always slips out of my hand and goes—**BANG!**"

"You should eat your roast beef, Mr. Flibberty-jib," said Mrs. Flibberty-jib, as she often did, "and wear your mittens."

"Nonsense!" shouted Mr. Flibberty-jib, giving his umbrella a good hard bump. "The noise! It's the noise!"

"Roast beef and mittens," said Mrs. Flibberty-jib.

"Noise!" roared Mr. Flibberty-jib.

This went on for days and days and days. Mrs. Flibberty-jib went on roasting the finest roast beef in the town. She went on making mittens—red mittens, blue mittens, yellow mittens.

Mr. Flibberty-jib's rumble in his head went on rumbling. At last Mr. Flibberty-jib came home in a rage.

"I can't stand this **rumble-rumble-rumble** and **bumble-bumble-bumble**," he said. "We will go to the country where it is quiet. Everyone knows the country is quiet and a very good place for rumbles and bumbles."

"Very well, Mr. Flibberty-jib," said Mrs. Flibberty-jib.

So Mr. Flibberty-jib packed up his brown shoes and his blue suit and his red tie. He put his hat over the rumble in his head. And he was ready to go to the country.

Mrs. Flibberty-jib packed up her roasting pans and her knitting needles and yarn. And she was ready to go to the country.

Poor Mr. Flibberty-jib! The train whistle said, **"TOOT, TOOT, TOOT,"** all the way to the country.

And every crossing bell said, "TING-ting-and-a-little-TING," all the way to the country.

But at last Mr. Flibberty-jib and Mrs. Flibberty-jib got to the country.

Mr. Flibberty-jib unpacked his brown shoes and his blue suit and his red tie and went for a quiet walk. Mrs. Flibberty-jib unpacked her roasting pans and her knitting needles and her yarn and began to cook a fine roast of beef.

They were so tired from all the packing and unpacking that they went to bed as soon as they had eaten supper.

"Oh, this is the life!" said Mr. Flibberty-jib, who hadn't eaten any of the roast beef.

Poor Mr. Flibberty-jib! He had just turned off the light and closed his eyes, when—

"**Whoo? Who? Who?**"

Poor, poor Mr. Flibberty-jib!

He was sure he had just hopped into bed.

He was sure he had just gone to sleep.

He was sure it was just the beginning of the night, when—

"Cock-a-doodle-doo!
Cock-a-doodle-doo!"

Mr. Flibberty-jib ran down the stairs and out of the house.

"Ssh! Sssh!" he said to the rooster. "I am a poor man with a rumble and bumble in my head."

"Cock-a-doodle-doo!"

shouted the rooster.

And the hens said,

"Cluck, cluck, cluck!"

"Oh, my!" cried Mr. Flibberty-jib. "What next?"

These were next:

"BOW, WOW, WOW!"

"Meow, meow, meow!"

Then the ducks came a-waddling to find a place for swimming. "QUACK, QUACK, QUACK!"

The old windmill turned and turned in the wind. It pumped water, and the horse came to drink.

"Squee-gee, squee-gee, squee-gee!" said the windmill. "I must turn and turn. Soon Bossy will come for her drink of cold water. Blow me around and around, Wind. *Squee-gee, squee-gee, squee-gee!"*

And the Bob White called from the green field,

"BOB WHITE! BOB WHITE!"

The big Bossy cow said, **"MOO-OOO! MOO-OO!"** It was time for milking!

The pails went **CLANK-CLANKETY-CLANK** as the farmer's biggest boy carried them into the barn.

And Mr. Flibberty-jib's head went **rumble-rumble-rumble** from his left ear to his right ear, and **bumble-bumble-bumble** from his right ear to his left ear.

"Less noise!" shouted Mr. Flibberty-jib.

"More roast beef," said Mrs. Flibberty-jib. "And your mittens."

"Well, now, it may be that you are right," said Mr. Flibberty-jib. "I hope so, for I have found that, town or country, there will always be—

NOISES! NOISES! NOISES!

So Mr. Flibberty-jib sat down at the table, and first he ate a small piece of roast beef and then a very large piece of roast beef.

And in the afternoon he was pleased to find that the **bumble-bumble-bumble** was gone from his head.

The next day he ate two very large pieces of roast beef and a slice of bread covered with rich brown gravy.

When he went outdoors, he wore the red-and-yellow mittens Mrs. Flibberty-jib had very kindly made for him.

And he was pleased to find that the **rumble rumble rumble** was gone from his head.

"Fine place, the country," said Mr. Flibberty-jib that night as he watched the big round moon.

He listened to the owl asking, **"Who? Whoo?"**

And not a **bumble-bumble-bumble** did Mr. Flibberty-jib hear.

"Fine place, the country," said Mr. Flibberty-jib next morning, and he jumped out of bed before the sun was up.

When the black rooster hurried sleepily to the fence to crow the sun up, there was Mr. Flibberty-jib.

"Cock-a-doodle-doo!"

"Listen to me try it," said Mr. Flibberty-jib.

"COCK-A-DOODLE-DOO!"

"Very good," said the black rooster. "Now listen to me."

He took a deep, DEEP breath.

"COCK-A-DOODLE-DOO!"

And not a **rumble-rumble-rumble** did Mr. Flibberty-jib hear.

Now Mr. Flibberty-jib and Mrs. Flibberty-jib go to the country every summer, and to the big city every winter.

And from that day to this, Mr. Flibberty-jib has always eaten plenty of roast beef, and he always wears his red-and-yellow mittens—except, of course, when he is eating roast beef.

And not a **rumble rumble rumble**—or a **bumble-bumble-bumble**—does Mr. Flibberty-jib ever hear.

The NEW BABY

By RUTH *and* HAROLD SHANE

Illustrated by ELOISE WILKIN

Mike lived in a white house. There was a green lawn around the house, and lots of pretty flowers.

Mike was sweeping the garage. Daddy was mowing the lawn. Mummy was in the house cooking supper.

A big red truck stopped in front of the house. The delivery man took a large box from the truck. He was bringing it to Mike's house.

What could it be? It wasn't Christmas, so it couldn't be a Christmas present. It wasn't a lawn mower. Daddy had a lawn mower. It wasn't a new tricycle. Mike had a new red tricycle. "Hello," Mike said to the delivery man.

"Hello, there," said the delivery man.

"Is that for us?" asked Mike.

"Yes," replied the delivery man. He rang the doorbell.

"What's in the box?" Mike asked.

"It's a bathinette."

Mike wondered what a bathinette could be.

Mummy came to the door. "Please bring the box right in," she said to the man.

The delivery man put the box by the window. Then he went back to the truck and drove away.

Mike looked at the big box. "What's a bathinette, Mummy?" he asked.

Daddy came in before Mummy had time to answer. "Aha!" he said. "Here's our new bathinette."

"What IS a bathinette?" asked Mike again.

"A bathinette is a baby's bathtub," Daddy told Mike. "It's for the new baby."

For a minute Mike did not say anything.

"Whose baby?" he asked at last.

"OUR baby," Daddy said. "After a while we're going to have a new, little one."

Mike couldn't believe it!

"A BABY!" he said excitedly. "What will it be like?

"Will it be a little girl?

"Will it be a boy?

"When is it coming here?

"Will it have red hair like Susie next door?"

"Hold on a minute!" laughed Daddy. "We don't know what it will look like or whether it will be a little boy or a little girl. We can only guess. It's a surprise!"

"When will the baby be here?" Mike asked.

Daddy told Mike that the baby would come quite soon.

Then Mummy said, "Time for supper!" before Mike could ask one more question.

Mike ate a big supper and he had a cookie for dessert. And all the time he wondered what the baby would be like, and thought of the fun he could have with a baby brother or sister.

A few days later Mike had another surprise. Aunt Pat was coming. Daddy, Mummy, and Mike went to the station to meet her.

"Aunt Pat is going to help you and Mummy feed and bathe the baby," said Daddy as they watched the train pull into the station.

"There's Aunt Pat," Mike cried.

The first thing Aunt Pat said was, "How big you are, Mike!"

The first thing Mike said was, "We're going to have a baby!"

"Is that so!" said Aunt Pat. She seemed very surprised.

"Yes! And you and I are going to help feed it!'

"Well, well!" said Aunt Pat.

She still looked very surprised.

At supper Mike asked, "Who will bring the baby?"

Daddy said, "No one will bring it. Mummy will go to hospital for the baby."

"Yes," Mummy explained. "In a little while the doctor will help me have the baby at the hospital."

"Aunt Pat, Mummy's going to have the baby at the hospital," Mike repeated.

That night Mike woke up. The light was burning. It was still dark outside. Aunt Pat was in the hall. She wore her bathrobe. Mummy and Daddy were up, too.

"Where are you going?" Mike asked.

Mummy kissed Mike and smiled. "I'm going to the hospital for our baby," she said. "I'll bring it home soon."

In the morning Mike helped Aunt Pat. He laced his shoes. He brought out the corn flakes. He carried chairs to the table. He brought in the milk. And he ate every bit of his breakfast.

The telephone rang. Mike got there first. It was Daddy.

Daddy said, "Mike, you have a fine baby sister!"

"Ohhh!" said Mike, handing the telephone to Aunt Pat. "Maybe I could run and tell Mrs. Blair."

"Of course you may," Aunt Pat told him.

So Mike ran next door as fast as he could.

Before long Daddy came home in the car. He boosted Mike in the air and then ran into the house to see Aunt Pat.

Just then a big red truck stopped in front of the house. The delivery man took a big box from the truck. He was bringing it to Mike's house. What could it be?

It wasn't Christmas yet, so it couldn't be a Christmas present. It couldn't be a lawn mower. Daddy still had a lawn mower. And it couldn't be a tricycle. Mike still had his red tricycle. Could it be another bathinette?

Mike ran up the steps. He didn't even wait to say "Hello" to the delivery man. He went looking for Daddy and Aunt Pat. He was quite excited.

"Aunt Pat," Mike said, "are we going to have ANOTHER baby?"

"What!" said Daddy.

"I hardly think so," said Aunt Pat. "At least not for a while. Why do you ask?"

"Well," said Mike, "the delivery man is here with another box. He brought one just before the baby came!"

Daddy laughed and said, "This is a surprise for YOU, Mikie. Let's go and get the package."

The delivery man was at the door.

"Hello," Mike said.

"Hello, there," said the delivery man.

"That's for ME," Mike told him and pointed to the big package. Daddy and the delivery man carried the box up the stairs.

"What can it be?" Mike wondered. "It's too big to be toys."

"Come on!" said Daddy.

"Give me a hand and soon you'll see what it is."

Mike ran upstairs. He and Daddy opened the box and there—was a big new bed!

"For me!" cried Mike.

Mike and Daddy put it together. Mike was very happy, and said, "NOW the baby can have my little bed!"

He wanted very much to see the baby.

It seemed a very long time that he had to wait. Aunt Pat and Daddy went to see Mummy and the baby every day.

Mike spent the days finding some of his toys for the baby to play with when she came home. What *would* she be like?

"What will we call her?" he wondered.

Daddy and Mike decided to call the baby Pat after Aunt Pat.

All the time Mike wondered, Where will she want to play? What will the baby look like? When will Mummy and the baby come home?

Then one day Daddy was bringing Mummy and Pat home from the hospital in the car. Mike sat on the steps and waited for them. A green car came along. It was not the car that Mike was looking for. A yellow car came along. It was not the right car either.

Then a blue car turned the corner. That was their car.

Mike ran down the sidewalk to the car. Daddy got out first. He gave Mike an extra high boost in the air. Mummy kissed Mike and told him how extra glad she was to be home.

Mrs. Blair came over from the house next door. Mrs. Mooney and Mrs. Hansen walked over from their houses across the street. Everyone wanted to see little Pat.

But Mike wanted to see her most of all.

He looked. She had tiny hands, and she had blue eyes. She had soft yellow hair, just as he had thought she might.

When Aunt Pat, Daddy, little Pat, and Mummy were inside, Mike said, "May I hold our baby?"

"Of course you may," Mummy said.

So Mike sat on the couch. Then they put a big pillow on his lap and put the baby on the pillow. How proud Mike was! It's wonderful to have a baby, Mike decided.

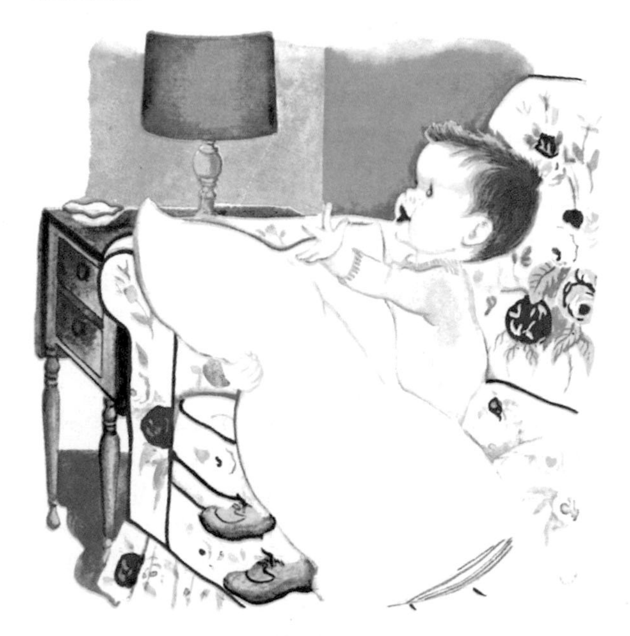

LITTLE **Peewee**

OR NOW OPEN THE BOX

By DOROTHY KUNHARDT

Illustrated by J. P. MILLER

Once there was a circus man with a quite tall red hat on his head and he had a circus of his very own so that was why he was called the circus man, and it was a very wonderful, wonderful circus.

The circus man kept his wonderful circus inside a big red tent.

Every day the circus man stood in front of his big red tent and every day he held up something in his hand very high for everybody to see. He held up a teeny weeny little box in his hand and he shouted very LOUD . . . Come on everybody come on over here to my tent come on everybody I have something exciting to show you just wait until I show you what I have in this little box so hurry up everybody and everybody came running and skipping and hopping as fast as they could to the circus man's big red tent and when everybody was there the circus man said . . . Everybody look now everybody look now everybody LOOK now everybody LOOK!

Then he opened the box and out came the teeniest-weeniest teeny teeny teeny weeny weeny weeny little dog in all the world and he was dear little Peewee the circus dog.

He just stepped out of his teeny weeny box and he looked around at everybody and the minute he looked around at everybody everybody loved him.

Then the circus man said Well I knew everybody would love my little Peewee it's too bad he doesn't know any tricks not a single one not even how to roll over not even how to shake hands but never mind he is so teeny weeny that everybody loves him. And that was true because EVERYBODY loved little Peewee.

There was the clown with two heads but one of them is probably make-believe.

He loved little Pee Wee.

There was the small man who could juggle three ducks all at the same time.

He loved little Peewee.

There was the man sitting on top of six tables just going to fall down and blowing soap bubbles. He loved little Peewee.

There was the lady standing on her head on an umbrella and with one foot she is holding a pair of scissors and with the other foot she is holding a cup full of nice warm milk. She loved little Peewee.

There was the elephant crawling under another elephant. He loved little Peewee.

There was the thin man. He loved little Peewee.

There was the strong baby holding up an automobile with a seal in the back seat. He loved little Peewee.

There was the snake that can put his tail in his mouth and then go rolling right up the stairs. He loved little Peewee.

There was the lady hanging in the air by just her nose being tied to a good strong rope. She loved little Peewee.

There was the fat lady. She loved little Peewee.

There was the polar bear who could jump in the air and click his ice skates together four times.

He loved little Peewee.

There was the goat that could stand right on a bed with the bed all burning up and not even mind about the fire being hot. He loved little Peewee.

There was the huge tall giant. He loved little Peewee.

But one day a terrible frightful awful thing happened. One day little teeny weeny weeny weeny Peewee started to grow

and he grew

and he grew

and he grew

until poor little Peewee the circus dog was just the same size as any other plain dog that you would see anywhere if you were looking at any plain dog and how could a circus man keep just a plain dog in his circus. Then the circus man cried and he said Now I can't keep you in my circus any more dear little Peewee and I am so sorry if only you could do some tricks it would be different but you can't do any tricks not even roll over not even shake hands and now you are just as big as any plain dog and how can I keep just a plain dog in my circus. NO I just can't so we must say goodbye dear little Peewee.

Then all the whole wonderful circus cried and the whole circus said Goodbye dear little Peewee.

So poor little Peewee started to go away and never come back to the circus any more and JUST THEN a wonderful splendid beautiful thing happened. Just as dear little Peewee was beginning to walk away so sadly and so slowly . . . he started to grow again!

And he grew

and he **grew**

and he **grew**

and then the circus man said Oh my dearest little Peewee now you won't have to go after all because now you are so lovely and big you are just the very dog for my circus! So little Peewee stayed in the circus man's wonderful circus and everybody loved him and everyday just before the circus started the circus man would stand outside the big red tent and beside him he would have a huge enormous box right beside him so everybody could see what a huge enormous box it was and then the circus man would shout Come on everybody come on over to my tent hurry up everybody I have something exciting to show you just wait till you see what I have in this great enormous box so hurry up everybody.

And everybody would come running and skipping and hopping to the circus man's wonderful circus tent and then the circus man would say Come on inside the tent everybody and I will open the box for you.

And then everybody would help the circus man push and push the great enormous box into the tent and then the circus man would open the top of the great enormous box and out would POP dear little Peewee and the circus man would say People this is my dear little circus dog Peewee and he is the hugest most enormous dog in the whole world and I love him dearly and every time the circus man said he is the hugest most enormous dog in the whole world and I love him dearly then little Peewee felt

VERY

HAPPY

INDEED!

BUSY TIMMY
By KATHRYN and
BYRON JACKSON
Illustrated by ELOISE WILKIN
1
Timmy is
a big boy.
2
He can put on his
outdoor clothes.
3
He can find his shovel
and his big sand pail.
4
He goes down the steps.
No one has to help him.
He's a big boy now.
5
He climbs in his sand-
box.
6
A robin sees Timmy and
comes flying.
7
A squirrel sees
Timmy and comes
running.
8
A rabbit sees Timmy
and comes hopping.
They all watch Timmy.

He makes little holes and big hills.
9
10
He rides on his horse all around the flower bed,
11
up bumps and down bumps
12
and back home again.
13
Timmy goes up the steps
14
and opens the door all by himself.
He gets ready for his bath.
15
No one has to help him. He's a big boy now.
16
He splashes in the bathtub, and sails his new boat.
17
He puts on his own bib,

18

and holds his own cup.

19

He eats all his supper
with no help at all.

20

He brushes
his own teeth.

21

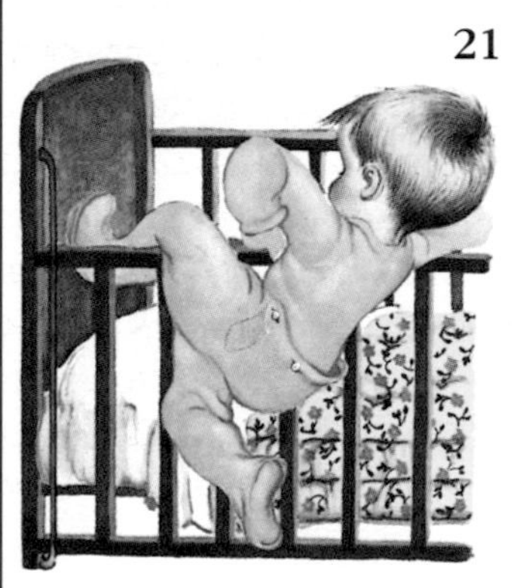

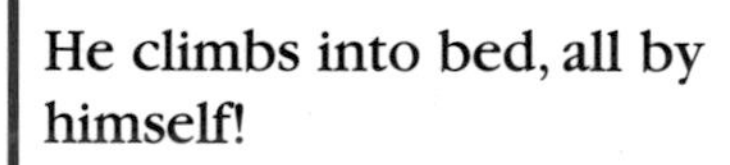

He climbs into bed, all by himself!

22

"Hush!" says the robin.

23

"Hush!" says the squirrel.

24

"Shush!" says the rabbit.
"Timmy is a big boy,
and Timmy is going to
sleep!"

25

Yes,
Timmy *is* a big boy—
and he is sound asleep.

26

You are big, too.
Timmy does a lot of things.
So can you!

A Year in the City

By LUCY SPRAGUE MITCHELL

Illustrated by TIBOR GERGELY

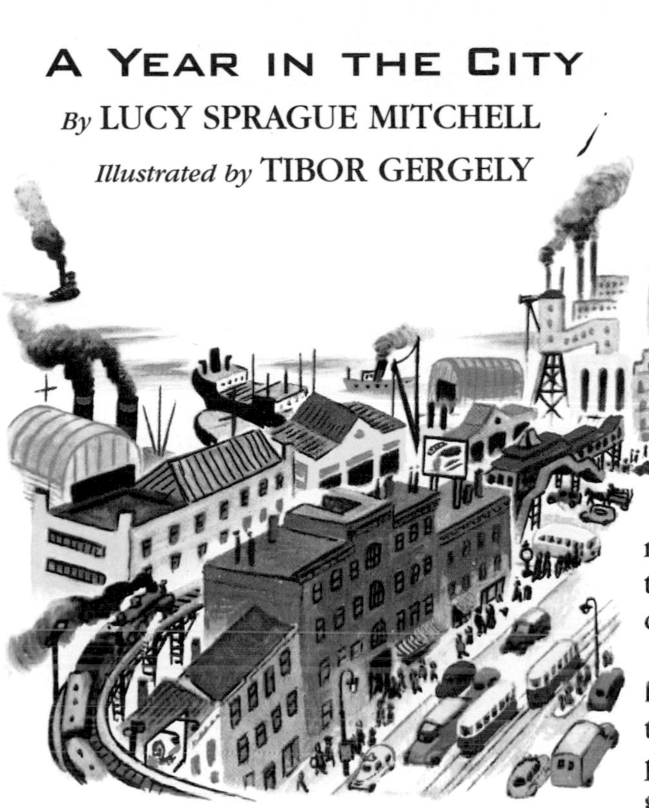

All year a city is a busy place. Autos honk on the streets. Boats toot in the harbor. Trains puff into the station. People's feet click along the sidewalks. Streetcars rattle down the streets. Airplanes whirr overhead. All year Billy and Jenny hear all these busy city sounds. Honk, honk! Toot, toot! Puff, puff! Click, click! Rattle, rattle! Whirrrrrr!

A city is full of busy people hurrying to work. Some work in stores selling things, some in factories making things. Some drive horses. Some drive trucks. Some drive buses. Some drive horse carts. Some drive engines. Some steer boats. Some pilot airplanes. Some build houses, or bridges. Some fix the pipes that run under the streets.

All year Jenny and Bill see all these busy city sights.

Near the river Jenny can see high chimneys. Smoke is always coming out of these chimneys, in spring, in summer, in fall, in winter. These are factory chimneys. Different factories make different things. Some make furniture. Some make clothes or shoes. Some make crackers.

Jenny lives high up in a big apartment house. She can watch the airplanes, and the boats in the harbor. She can hear the puffing trains all night. Billy lives on the ground floor next door to Jenny. He can see people and horses and buses on the street and men fixing the pipes under the streets. In spring, in summer, in fall, in winter, Billy and Jenny watch everything the busy city does.

SPRING TIME

Painters paint the railing red.
Tulips bloom in tulip bed,
Pushcart men with
flowers shout,
Hurdy gurdies
Wheel about.

Spring is the time that painters paint all outdoor iron—first red, then black or green or gray. Billy's front fence and the fire-escapes down the back of the house are painted. Jenny sees the painters paint the big bridge over the river. She and her mother buy peas and strawberries from a cart. "Flowers! flowers!" calls the man on Billy's street. Billy and his mother buy pots of geraniums for the window box.

Builders begin building in the spring. Across the street steam shovels dig a big hole. A cement mixer mixes cement and sharp stones. Then the men build the cement foundations. Big trucks bring great steel beams. Then rat-a-tat the riveters put in hot rivets to hold the beams together. Then come bricklayers and stone masons and carpenters, men with pipes and wires and plasterers and painters. The men begin building in the spring. They work all summer, too. Jenny and Billy watch and hear it all.

All year the busy trains bring milk from the farms to the city. Every morning the milkman leaves two bottles of milk at the door of Billy's house and two more at the door of Jenny's high-up apartment.

More busy trains bring flour and sugar, fruit and vegetables. All year round the grocery store near by is full of oranges and apples and fresh vegetables. Billy and Jenny help their mothers carry home big bundles of things that have been grown on some farm near at hand or far away.

Airplanes are winging over the city. Jenny hears them through her open window. They are high in the sky, much higher than Jenny's apartment. Down they swoop to the city's airport, with their passengers and mail. One day Billy's father takes Billy and Jenny to the airport to see the planes.

"When I'm big," says Billy, "I'll be a pilot."

"Maybe I'll be one, too," says Jenny.

SUMMER TIME

In the park the fountains play,
Children romp around all day,
Sprinkling carts come
Down the street
And cool the tired children's feet.

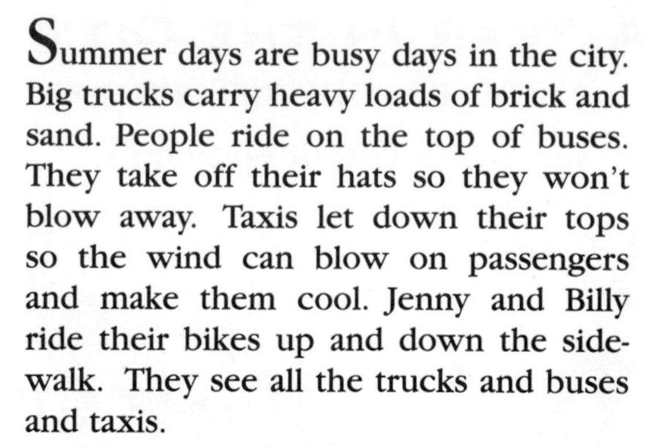

Summer days are busy days in the city. Big trucks carry heavy loads of brick and sand. People ride on the top of buses. They take off their hats so they won't blow away. Taxis let down their tops so the wind can blow on passengers and make them cool. Jenny and Billy ride their bikes up and down the sidewalk. They see all the trucks and buses and taxis.

The street cleaner on Jenny's and Billy's street trundles his can on wheels past their houses. He takes his stiff broom and sweeps the dirt and papers into a dust pan with a long handle. He dumps the stuff in his can and goes off down the street.

One day the sprinkling cart comes down the street. The water whooshes out on both sides and behind it and runs in little streams down into the gutter. Billy and Jenny are terribly hot. "The water looks cool," says Billy. Jenny kicks off her sandals. "Come on, Bill," she says. So they stand on the edge of the street and the cool water whooshes right over their hot feet.

A mother who lives across the street rolls a baby carriage out on the sidewalk. Billy and Jenny tiptoe close to the carriage and peek. There lies a baby with red cheeks sound asleep. His legs and feet and arms are bare.

One day some men come with sharp pickaxes and begin to tear up the street right in front of their houses. "What are you going to do?" asks Jenny.

"We're going to connect the pipes and wires in the new house with the pipes under the street," says the man.

"What comes in those pipes?" asks Billy.

"Water comes in some, gas comes in some. Some pipes have wires in them."

"What kind of wires?" asks Jenny.

"Wires for electricity so the new house can have electric light and electric bells and heat for its stoves. Wires for the telephones. All these pipes and wires run under the streets all over the city. To every house."

The boats are busy in the summer. Jenny and Billy go for a ride on a ferry. They see a big steamer from far away steam into the harbor. They hear its deep low voice. "Toot! Toot!" it booms. All the boats in the harbor hurry to get out of the way of the big steamer. Jenny's and Billy's ferry hurries to get across the river. Fishing boats turn their sails and sail away. Tugs pulling barges steer away from the steamer. But six little tugs don't get out of the steamer's way. They have high quick voices. "Toot-oo-toot!" they scream. They chug up to the big steamer. Men on the tugs throw ropes to the men on the big steamer. Then the little tugs pull and push the big steamer into the dock.

Jenny and Billy go to the park every day in the summer. They ride their tricycles round and round the sidewalks in the park. They take turns pushing each other on the swings. They sail their boats in the water by the fountain. The wind blows the water of the fountain right over them. Jenny and Billy run around in the sun until they are dry.

In the park bloom flowers—red, white, orange and yellow. The grass is shady under the trees. Jenny and Billy lie down and look up. Jenny sees a yellow and black bird. Billy sees a squirrel with a long fluffy tail.

"A tree makes a nice cool home in the summer," says Jenny.

FALL TIME

Leaves are falling,
Nights are cool,
Bigger children go to school,
Coal goes rattling down the chute,
Time for warmer dress or suit.

Fall days grow chilly. The coal truck stops in front of Billy's house. Up goes the front of the truck. The coal rattles down a chute from the truck, through a hole in the sidewalk. Down into Billy's cellar, rattlety bang! Down into Jenny's cellar! Now they have coal to keep them warm through the winter.

The streets are full of moving vans in the fall. Vans stop in front of the new house. The men carry in the furniture.

In the fall the big children go off to school. Billy and Jenny walk as far as the school playground and watch the children go in. "Maybe next year we'll go," says Billy to Jenny.

"It's time for your warm dress, Jenny," says her mother. But Jenny's old dress is too small for her. And Billy's old suit is too small for him. Off they go to a big store. There they find lots of other children who are too big for their last year's clothes, just like Jenny and Billy.

It is snowing. The wind blows the snow against Jenny's window with little soft thuds. She can hardly see the new building across the street. When the sun comes out, Jenny sees snow over everything. The city is white and still. Off to the park go Jenny and Billy with their sleds. They coast down a little hill. They laugh and yell in the snow.

The snow lies thick on the city streets. The snow plow makes a growling noise scooping up the snow. Billy and Jenny hear the noise and run out to watch. Slowly the snow plow moves down the street. When it is gone, the autos can once more move along the street.

The snow lies thick on the railroad tracks. Down the tracks moves a snow plow pushed by an engine. It sends the snow flying off the tracks into big piles on one side. The tracks are clear. Down the tracks moves a milk train bringing milk to the city.

Billy sees the milk wagon stop in front of his house. He runs to the door. There is a milkman with two bottles of milk.

"I was afraid you wouldn't come today," said Billy. "There's so much snow." The milkman laughed. "It has to be a very big storm to keep the milk train from running!"

Then the Christmas trees begin to come to the city. They come from the country where the trees grow. They come on puffing trains. They come on trucks. The Christmas trees even come on boats.

Christmas trees stand in front of the city stores. Billy's father and Jenny's father each carries a Christmas tree home!

All the year round the mailman carries letters. He carries letters to Billy's house and to Jenny's house. In December the mailman's bag gets heavier and heavier. In his bag are boxes—little boxes and big boxes. Billy and Jenny put their boxes under the tree.

The harbor boats have a hard time in winter. The river is frozen over with ice. Ice cutters break the ice so the boats can move around. Floating ice bumps into the boats. The boats go slowly through the floating ice. Jenny watches them from her high-up window. She hears them toot and whistle.

"They sound mad at the ice," thinks Jenny.

WINTER TIME

Snow plows clear away the snow,
Autos skid unless they're slow,
The river's full of floating ice,
And Christmas trees on streets smell nice.

THE GOLDEN
Sleepy Book

By MARGARET WISE BROWN

Illustrated by GARTH WILLIAMS

THE WHISPERING RABBIT

Once there was a sleepy little rabbit
Who began to yawn—
And he yawned and he yawned and he yawned and he yawned,
"Hmmm———"

He opened his little rabbit mouth when he yawned till you could see his white front teeth and his little round pink mouth, and he yawned and he yawned until suddenly a bee flew into his mouth and he swallowed the bee.

"Hooo— hoo—," said a fat old owl. "Always keep your paw in front of your mouth when you yawn," hooted the owl.

"Rabbits never do that," said the sleepy little rabbit.

"Silly rabbits!" said the owl and he flew away.

The little rabbit was just calling after him, but when the little rabbit opened his mouth to speak, the bumblebee had curled up to sleep in his throat——AND ——all he could do was whisper.

"What shall I do?" he whispered to a squirrel who wasn't sleepy.

"Wake him up," said the squirrel. "Wake up the bumblebee."

"How?" whispered the rabbit. "All I can do is whisper and I'm sleepy and I want to go to sleep and who can sleep with a bumblebee—"

Suddenly a wise old groundhog popped up out of the ground.

"All I can do is whisper," said the little rabbit.

"All the better," said the groundhog.

"Come here, little rabbit," he said, "and I will whisper to you how to wake up a bumblebee.

"You have to make the littlest noise that you can possibly make because a bumblebee doesn't bother about big noises. He is a very little bee and he is only interested in little noises."

"Like a loud whisper?" asked the rabbit.

"Too loud," said the groundhog and popped back into his hole.

"A little noise," whispered the rabbit and he started making little rabbit noises—he made a noise as quiet as the sound of a bird's wing cutting the air, but the bee didn't wake up. So the little rabbit made the sound of snow falling but the bee didn't wake up.

So the little rabbit made the sound of a bug breathing and a fly sneezing and grass rustling and a fireman thinking. Still the bee didn't wake up. So the rabbit sat and thought of all the little sounds he could think of—What could they be?

A sound quiet as snow melting, quiet as a flower growing, quiet as an egg, quiet as—And suddenly he knew the little noise that he would make—and he made it.

It was like a little click made hundreds of miles away by a bumblebee in an apple tree in full bloom on a mountain top. It was the very small click of a bee swallowing some honey from an apple blossom.

And at that the bee woke up.

He thought he was missing something and away he flew.

And then what did the little rabbit do? That sleepy sleepy little rabbit?

He closed his mouth
He closed his eyes
He closed his ears
And he tucked in his paws
And twitched his nose
And he went sound asleep!

Once there was a bunny who liked only the very early morning. He loved the first rays of the round sun square on his nose. He loved the frost that made the world look like the dream he had just been having of a glass forest. Early in the morning the big leaves of the sassafras were etched in white—the blades of grass shiny and brittle with ice and the feathery flowering grasses glassy and sparkling like diamonds. So, in some magic way, the little bunny felt still a part of his dreams in the morning.

But later, when the rays of the big round sun fell on the tree tops and the mother bunnies began calling their babies to help them wash up, then, oh, then the little bunny would go and hide in the immense folding leaves of a cabbage. He was so little he could sit inside a cabbage and peek out through the immense folding leaves.

And because he went on like this he was called the Bunny No Good.

When the other little bunnies were hopping about doing their work, there was the Bunny No Good sitting in a cabbage.

But, do you know, he never missed a thing.

He wasn't really sleeping, he was just a dreamy bunny.

And his little red ruby eyes blinked out of his square fur face and they never missed a trick. He saw the spiders spin their webs and he watched the foolish flies fly into them. He saw the mole start

down a long hole to go off far down his tunnel and dig under someone's flat green lawn. He saw the other rabbits jumping about and running in circles and he knew all their funny little wiggles. The way they twitched their whiskers, the way they kicked sideways and wiggled their noses and thumped the earth with their hind legs when they were startled. And he made a dreamy little song to himself about rabbits:

Grow, grow.
Eat and grow.
What for
Rabbits never know.

Whiskers whisk,
Twitch, twitch the nose.
So red the eye, a ruby glows
Shinier than a wet, red rose
In a rabbit's face.

All this time there was another little rabbit who went hopping about bright as a button, merry as a cricket, fit as a fiddle, busy as a beaver, and keen as a whistle.

His name was Bunny Bun Bun. And his big fat mother looked down her soft fur face and said to the other eleven hundred little rabbits, "Look at Bunny Bun Bun. If you all want to be as bright as a button, merry as a cricket, fit as a fiddle, busy as a beaver, and keen as a whistle, just do as Bunny Bun Bun does."

All this time the Bunny No Good was singing and dreaming and blinking away to himself in the immense folding leaves of a cabbage.

He watched a flock of wild black crows go flying through the sky screaming their awful wild crow music.

He watched them light in an old fat oak tree, making a crown of crows on the topmost branches.

All this was still very early in the morning.

Some of the frost had been melted into shiny, wet water by the sun. Where the trees cast their shadows there was a shadow of frost on the ground, a white shadow away from the sun, a white triangle shadow for the pine trees and the holly bushes, and a great spreading feathery shadow for the other trees.

All this the Bunny No Good noticed as he dreamed away the bright early morning minutes in his cabbage.

But not Bunny Bun Bun and the eleven hundred other little scurrying rabbits. They were too busy bustling about washing and dusting and making little straw bunny beds and sweeping and polishing and peeling carrots for lunch.

They did not notice the shadow of frost beneath the trees or the crown of crows in the old oak at the edge of the wood. They did not listen to the wild crow music. They were too busy about their own little bunny business.

And so they did not notice that the crows all rose in a wild black scatter from the branches of the tree and flapped and circled like heavy black shadows in the sky. They did not notice that the wild crow music grew wilder. They did not hear the screaming crows.

But the Bunny No Good did. All this he saw and heard as he dreamed in the immense folding leaves of the cabbage. He knew something was happening. And sure enough . . .

There came sneaking through the corn field a red fox.

The crows saw him, and the Bunny No Good saw the crows. Should he get down out of his cabbage and thump his hind legs on the ground to warn the other eleven hundred little bunnies?

Not yet.

It was still early in the morning.

He made a song to himself about crows:

Crows crows
Old black crows
Nobody knows
Where the red fox goes
Nobody knows
But the wild black crows.

The crows circled black across the sky, leaving the tree tops empty.

The fox came sniffing along and he saw nothing but eleven hundred little rabbit tracks and little holes in the ground, so he went away. And pretty soon Bunny Bun Bun poked his head out and saw that the fox was gone and even his scent had blown away across the land after him.

So he told the others, and eleven hun-

dred little bunny heads popped out of their holes and soon they were all hopping about as usual.

The red fox came creeping through, one paw lifted and another paw down, sniffing the cold moist air, delicately sniffing the breeze on which he could smell eleven hundred warm little rabbits.

This was no dream.

The Bunny No Good jumped out of his cabbage. He banged his hind legs thump on the ground—thump—then he ran like a weasel to the other eleven hundred little bunnies and they all dove head first into their holes in the ground where they were safe.

"Someone saved our lives," squeaked the eleven hundred little rabbits.

"Bravo!" called Bunny Bun Bun.

"Caw-Caw-Caw," screeched the crows.

But the Bunny No Good had gone back to his cabbage. His little red eyes blinked dreamily in his square fur face. And there he sat dreaming away in the immense folding leaves of the cabbage.

It was still very early in the morning.

RABBIT

POEM

Nobody knows a rabbit's nose
The way it twitches
The way it goes
Constantly on his face

Nobody knows a rabbit's ears
The way he listens
And what he hears
And his sad little rabbit
tears

Nobody knows a rabbit's eyes
Red as rubies without surprise
In his square fur face

CLOSE YOUR EYES

Little donkey on the hill
Standing there so very still
Making faces at the skies
Little donkey close your eyes.

Silly sheep that slowly crop
Night has come and you must stop
Chewing grass beneath the skies
Silly sheep now close your eyes.

Little monkey in a tree
Swinging there so merrily
Throwing coconuts at the skies
Little monkey close your eyes.

Little birds that sweetly sing
Curve your heads beneath your wing
No more whistling in the skies
Little birds now close your eyes.

Little horses in your stall
Stop your stomping, stop it all
Tails stop switching after flies
Little horses close your eyes.

Little pigs that snuff about
No more snorting with your snout
No more squealing to the skies
Noisy pigs now close your eyes.

Old black cat down in the barn
Keeping four black kittens warm
Winds are quiet in the skies
Dear old black cat close your eyes.

Little child all tucked in bed
Looking like a sleepy head
Stars are quiet in the skies
Little child now close your eyes.

All over the world the animals are going to sleep—the birds and the bees, the horse, the butterfly and the cat.

In their high nests by the ocean the fish hawks are going to sleep. And how does a young fish hawk go to sleep? The same as any other bird in the world.

He folds his wings and pushes himself deep in the nest, looks around and blinks his eyes three times, takes one long last look over the ocean, then tucks his head under his wing and sleeps in like a bird.

And the fish in the sea sleep in the darkened sea when the long green light of the sun is gone.

And they sleep like fish, with their eyes wide open in some quiet current of the sea.

And above and beyond under the stars on the land all the little horses are going to sleep. Some stand up in the still dark fields and some fold their legs under them and lie down. But they all go to sleep like horses.

And the old fat bear in the deep dark woods goes into his warm cave to sleep for the whole winter.

Even the bees and the butterflies sleep when the moths begin to fly. And they sleep like bees and butterflies under a leaf or a stick or a stone with folded wings and their eyes wide open. For fish and bees and butterflies and flies never close their shiny eyes.

So do the groundhogs and the hedgehogs, the skunks and the black-eyed raccoons. They eat a lot, then sleep until spring, a long warm sleep.

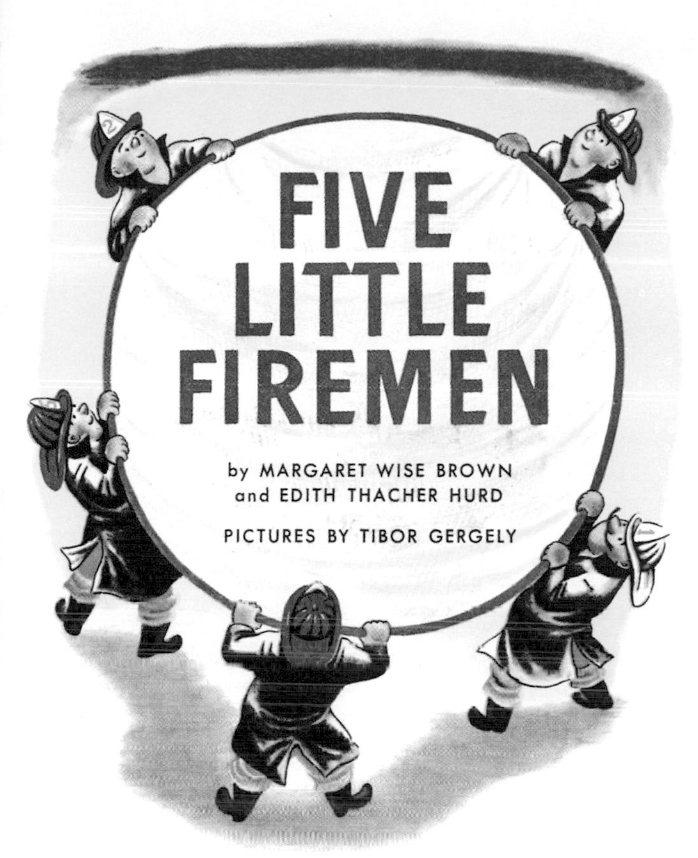

FIVE LITTLE FIREMEN

by MARGARET WISE BROWN
and EDITH THACHER HURD

PICTURES BY TIBOR GERGELY

A little house caught on fire.

The fire started so quietly, and it was such a little fire at first.

A flame like a little mouse came darting in and out of a hole in the hall closet and darted back again. A policeman smelled it.

But it grew and sizzled, and the house began to smoke, and the smoke blew out the window.

And then the policeman saw it. He peeked in the cellar window and saw the yellow flames in the gray smoke.

So he ran to the corner, opened the red alarm box, and called the Fire Department. Then he went back to the little house.

Ding, ding, ding—

Five little firemen slide down the firehouse pole.

"Sparks!" shouts the First Little Fireman.

He puts on his white helmet, twirls his black mustache, and jumps into the little red Chief's car with its shiny brass bell. Cling, clang!

The First Little Fireman has to be the first at the fire, to tell the other firemen what to do when they get there.

He is the fire chief.

"A fire won't wait," says the Second Little Fireman. Round as a pumpkin, he jumps into the driver's seat of the hook-and-ladder truck, the biggest fire engine of all.

"We'll save all the people," says the Third Little Fireman.

The Third Little Fireman jumps on the side of the hook-and-ladder truck as it rolls out the door. He has muscles as big as baseballs, he is that strong. He runs up the ladders and carries the people down the ladders—that Third Little Fireman.

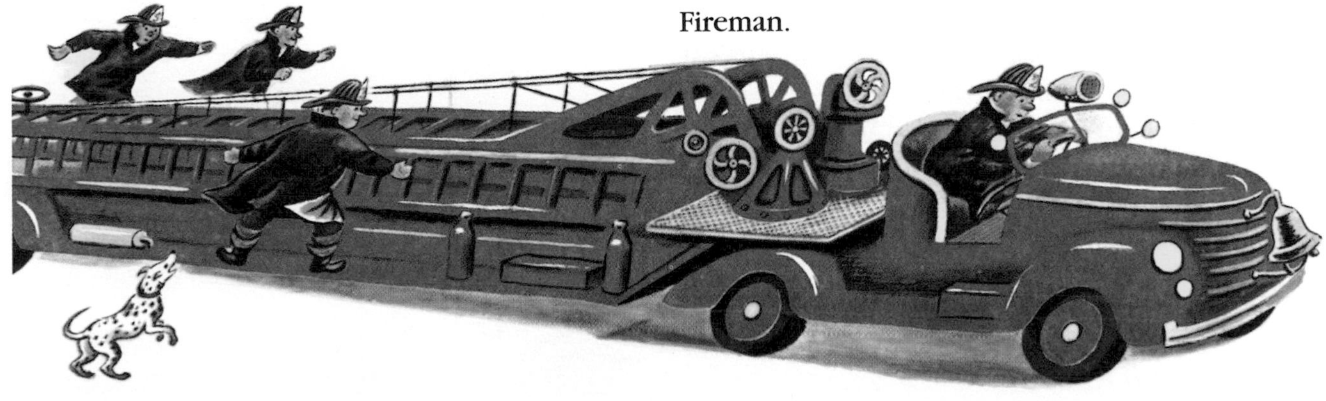

"We'll squirt lots of water," says the Fourth Little Fireman, who is bright as a button and so drives the huge tower truck.

"I sneeze in the smoke," says the Fifth Little Fireman. Spry as a fly, he jumps on his hose truck and roars out the firehouse door.
With a clang, cling, clang
and a Wheeeeeeeee
and a Whoooooooo
The tires of the trucks go hissing around,
leaving the firehouse behind.
Clang, cling, clang—the Chief's bell.
Whee-ee, whee-ee, whee-ee—the tower truck's siren.
Dong, dong, dong, the hose truck skids around the corner.
Whoooooooooooooooooo, wails the long hook-and-ladder truck, the biggest fire engine of them all.
Get out of the way!
Here come the Five Little Firemen.
With a clang, cling, clang,
and a Wheeeeeeeee
and a Whoooooooooooo
they go whizzing up a street called
Oak Street
then whizzing
around a corner into $12\frac{1}{2}$ Street
down Asphalt Avenue
then down Eucalyptus Drive
and up the King's Highway
and over Baseball Boulevard
to Small Bush Road.
Dong, dong, dong.

And there on Small Bush Road was the little house on fire.

Flames the size of pocket handkerchiefs were waving out of the windows. And lots of smoke!

When the policeman got to the door, the door was on fire.

"Chop it down," he ordered.

But he kicked it down with his foot and ran upstairs and woke up a very sleepy family, who all started sneezing with the smoke.

This was the Hurricane Jones Family, and they were terribly sleepy.

"Grab what you love most and run out of your house," ordered the policeman.

Mrs. Hurricane Jones tried to grab her three little boys and run out of the house with them; but when she went to grab them, the first little boy had run to grab his cat, the second little boy had run downstairs and out of the house to take care of his rabbits, and the third little boy had grabbed all the flowers that he had picked the day before and was halfway down the stairs with them.

So Mrs. Hurricane Jones, still very sleepy, threw her mirrors out the window and picked up her pillow and ran downstairs.

Mr. Hurricane Jones grabbed his pipe and his matches and came afterwards to be sure that all his family were out of the house and standing in a line on the lawn.

And there they were, all safely out on their front lawn, each holding in his arms what he loved most, when the firemen came along.

But where is Hurricane Jones's jolly fat cook?

The Five Little Firemen, brave as can be, get to work.

The First Fireman yells more orders.

The Third Fireman rushes off to find the cook.

The Second Fireman backs the hook-and-ladder truck into just the right place. The Hurricane Jones's house is too tiny for big ladders. So he takes one of the little ladders and puts it up to the side of the house.

The Fourth Little Fireman points the water tower at the flames and squirts.

And the Fifth Little Fireman unrolls the hose and screws it onto the red fire hydrant. He turns it on and water that runs under the streets in big pipes all the time rushes through the hose.

Sh-sh-sh it squirts out of the nozzle like a roaring river through the air.

Swishhsh—they smash in the windows to let out the smoke.

And swishhsh—in roars the water to put out the flames.

The smoke gets all brown and yellow when the water hits it.

They chop down the burning wood and throw fireproof blankets over the furniture.

The Third Little Fireman has found the cook and he wants to carry her down the ladder on his back in the fireman's carry. "Nix," says she.

She is too fat to carry and too big to jump into a net and too jolly to stay and burn up in the flames.

So they shoot up the life-line for the Hurricane Jones's jolly fat cook to slide down.

And down she comes.

"Jewallopers!" says she. "It was getting warm up there."

And soon all the bright flames were wet black ashes and the crackling sound of the flames was quiet and there was only the great purring of the red hose truck pumping water and the bright searchlights of the fire engines making the trees and the bushes much greener than they had been before. The fire was over, and the Hurricane Jones Family went home with their Uncle Clement to sleep and to wait for their house to be fixed.

"Fire's out," calls the Chief, and that First Little Fireman climbs into his shiny red car.

"Let's go," says the Second Little Fireman.

"That was some cook," says the Third Little Fireman.

"Some fire!" says the Fourth Little Fireman.

"Kerchew," says the Fifth Little Fireman, as he rolls in his hose.

Then the engines back up, turn around, roar, and go away.

Only their bells clang slowly now, Clang, Cling, Clong, and a ding, ding, ding, they all go back to the firehouse.

The Five Little Firemen have black on their faces and black on their hands. The Chief's mustache is blacker than ever.

Their rubber coats and helmets are shiny wet with water from the hose.

The Five Little Firemen are tired.

"That's that," says the First Little Fireman.

"Whow," says the Second Little Fireman.

"Whee," says the Third Little Fireman.

"Whew," says the Fourth Little Fireman.

"Home!" says the Fifth Little Fireman. They have to wash the fire engines. Then they polish the bells and the sirens and all their equipment to be ready for another fire alarm at any minute, should one come.

At last the Five Little Firemen hang up their helmets and black rubber coats. They wash their hands and faces. There is no other fire alarm that night.

So the Five Little Firemen sit down to supper and sing songs and laugh and eat a lot of Irish stew.

There never are many fires. That is why the Five Little Firemen are so fat—all but one.

Five Little Firemen jump into bed.
Five Little Firemen,
Brave as can be,
Sleep, and they dream
Of the beautiful sea.

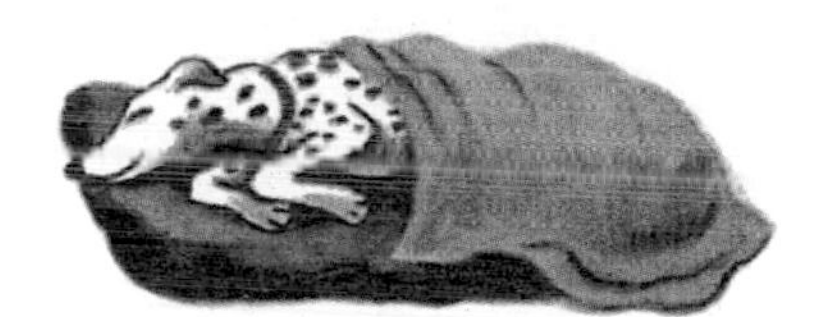

A NAME FOR *Kitty*

By PHYLLIS McGINLEY

Illustrated by

FEODOR ROJANKOVSKY

Once, on a farm in the country, there lived a little boy who was given a brand-new kitty to be his very own. But she had no name and the little boy didn't know what to call her.

So he went to his mother and asked, "Mother, what shall I call my kitty?"

Now his mother was busy icing a cake and she gave the little boy the beater to lick.

"Why don't you call her 'Tiger'?"

"Oh, no," said the little boy, "I can't call her 'Tiger.' She's not that big."

So he went to find his father.

"Father," he asked, "what shall I call my kitty?"

Now his father was busy mending a fence and he gave the little boy a hammer to hold while he put a board in place.

"Why don't you call her 'Shoe-leather,' because she's bound to be always under foot?"

"Oh, no!" cried the little boy. "That name's too long."

So he turned back to the house to find his grandfather.

His grandfather was sitting on the porch and he wasn't busy at all.

"Grandfather," asked the little boy, "what shall I call my kitty?"

"Wait a jiffy until I get my Thinking Cap," said his grandfather.

And he went inside to get his bright red Thinking Cap.

"Why don't you call her 'Joseph,' because he had a coat of many colors?"

"But 'Joseph' is a boy's name and this is a girl kitty," said the little boy.

The little boy wandered back down the path.

"If my mother doesn't know and my father doesn't know and neither does my grandfather," the little boy said to himself, "perhaps I could find out from the animals on the farm."

So he went to the stile and he climbed right over, and he asked of the cow who was nibbling at the clover,

"Cow, what shall I call my kitty?"

"Mooo," lowed the cow, shaking her horn at a butterfly. "Moo, moo-ooooo."

"Moo!" said the little boy. "That's no name for a kitty."

So he hurried to the barnyard as fast as he was able, and he asked of the horse, at dinner in the stable, "Horse, what shall I call my kitty?"

"Neigh," whinnied the horse, politely looking up from his oats. "Neigh, neighhhhh."

"Neigh!" exclaimed the little boy. "*That's* no name for a kitty."

So he walked by the garden, all alone, and he asked of the dog who was digging up a bone, "Dog, what shall I call my kitty?"

The dog stopped scraping for a minute.

"Bow-wow, bow-wow-wow," he barked.

"Bow-wow. Bow-wow, indeed!" cried the little boy crossly.

"That's no name at all for a kitty."

So he crossed the pasture to the hill below, and he asked of the sheep who were grazing in a row, "Sheep, what shall I call my kitty? "

"Baa," bleated all the sheep, raising their heads all in the same direction at the same time. "Baa."

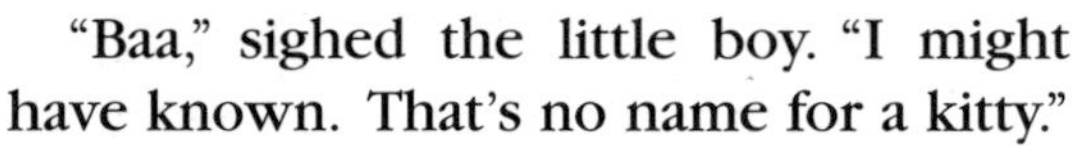

"Baa," sighed the little boy. "I might have known. That's no name for a kitty."

So he went to the chickens to try his luck, but the chicks said, "Peep," and the hens said, "Cluck."

And "Quack," said the duck when he asked the duck.

"Cooo," said the pigeon and "Coo," again.

"Gobble," said the turkey.

"Twitter," said the wren.

And the pig just grunted as if he hadn't heard.

And the fish in the fish pond *didn't say a word.*

So the little boy sat down sadly on the back doorstep in the sunlight and put his chin in his hands, and he thought and he thought and he thought.

The kitty chased a sunbeam and purred.

"Kitty," murmured the little boy. "Nice kitty. Here, kitty, kitty, kitty."

And then all of a sudden he jumped up.

"I know!" he shouted happily. "*I* know what I'll call my kitty. I'll call her 'Kitty.'"

And he did.

The Marvelous MERRY-GO-ROUND

By JANE WERNER

Illustrated by J. P. MILLER

There was once a little boy named Tommy Alan, who loved to ride on merry-go-rounds.

He even made himself a song about them, and he sang it every day. This was his song:

Someday I'll get me a merry-go-round
With a musical middle machine
And a beautiful canopy over the top
That is patterned in purple and green.
I'll be the man with the flashing white smile
And the shirtsleeves rolled up and no tie.
I will jump off and on as the platform goes round
And the animals all hurry by.

What a surprise for the children who come,
For they'll find when they finally arrive,
Instead of wood horses some gay kangaroos
And camels and llamas and zebras and moose,
And of course they will all be alive.
Yes, of course they will all be alive.

Whenever grownups asked, "And what are you going to be when you grow up?" the other children would say "a fireman" or "policeman" or "streetcar conductor." But not Tommy.

"I'm going to have me a merry-go-round," Tommy always said.

"And what's more," he added, half to himself, "the animals will all be alive."

Now through the years Tommy Alan stuck to his merry-go-round. All the other children switched from wanting to be firemen and policemen to airplane pilots, candy store owners, and cowboys.

And as time went by a lot of them grew up to find that they had turned into business men and lawyers and doctors instead of what they really had wanted to be.

But not Tommy Alan. The very morning Tommy was grown up, he went out and bought a merry-go-round. Yes, sir, a merry-go-round with a musical middle machine and a beautiful canopy over the top that was patterned in purple and green.

But even that was not enough for Tommy.

"None of these wooden animals for me," said Tommy. "On my merry-go-round they must be alive. Yes, of *course* they will be alive!"

So Tommy Alan went down to the zoo, and he bought all the beasts he would need.

"Now," said Tommy Alan, when he had shown them all to their places on the merry-go-round, "this is something like it!"

And as he turned the switch to start the machine, Tommy was cheerily whistling his old tune.

"What a surprise it will be for the children who come—" Tommy whistled.

The surprise, alas, was for Tommy! The children were delighted with the merry-go-round.

But when children go someplace, grownups, you know, almost always insist upon being taken along.

And the grownups were horrified.

For the giraffe could not resist nibbling at the fruit and flowers on the ladies' hats—though he found the flavor very disappointing.

And the camel grinned an evil grin—as only a camel can!—whenever a grownup came near.

Then when the moose gave a great moose bellow, just by way of welcome, that was the finish!

With little screams, squawks and cries, the grownups whisked all those children away.

And there was Tommy Alan with his very wonderful merry-go-round and all the real live animals, and not a soul to ride.

Not a single child was permitted to come back, though Tommy played all the prettiest tunes on his music machine, and the animals were on their best behavior.

"Oh, me!" sighed Tommy gloomily, as he sat with his head in his hands. "This is no fun at all."

"We will move to another town," said Tommy at last, looking firm. "We will try again!"

So away they went, and morning found Tommy and his merry-go-round in the next town.

The animals had just taken their places when the children began to arrive, with their grownups, of course, following close behind.

"Now we must be on our best behavior," Tommy whispered to his animals.

So they all tucked back their ears and put on their widest smiles. And all went well until—

"My," said one lady to the lady beside her, "the coat on this zebra looks so real, you would almost think it was alive, wouldn't you." And she pinched the zebra.

Well, he jumped, naturally enough, and gave a startled whinny, and the camel bared his yellow teeth and made an ugly sound. And the hippopotamus grunted a grunt that came right up from his toes.

That was the finish again. Quick as scat, off went those grownups, hustling the children before them.

And Tommy and his animals were left alone again.

Not a child came back for a single ride, though Tommy and the animals waited all day.

So that night they moved to the *next* town.

"This is our last chance," said Tommy. "We'll make the grownups think you are wooden animals."

"Oh, the children will still know you are real," Tommy promised them.

But the animals could not help wondering.

The animals looked sad as Tommy gave them all a coat of shiny wood-type paint.

They did not have long to worry, though, for the shiny paint was no more than dry when along came the children, bringing their grownups behind them.

"What a charming merry-go-round," said all the grownups, as they lifted their smallest children onto the hippopotamus's lovely wide back. "What interesting wooden animals. How very unusual," they said. "Isn't it quaint?"

The animals all stood like chunks of wood. But the children understood at once.

"They're alive!" they whispered under cover of the tinkling tunes from Tommy Alan's music machine. "How wonderful!"

And they fondly patted the animals' heads, and spoke to them as they rode. The animals flickered their ears ever so softly, to show that they had heard, and they smiled with their big, round eyes.

The grownups never guessed, though, so now Tommy Alan's troubles were ended.

Each day more children come to ride on his wonderful merry-go-round, as Tommy and his animals move from city to village to town.

And the grownups look at the animals and say, "How charming! How quaint!"

But the children know—yes, of course they do—the children know they're alive!

GASTON AND JOSEPHINE

By GEORGES DUPLAIX

Illustrated by

FEODOR ROJANKOVSKY

Gaston and his sister Josephine, two very rosy French pigs, lived with their mother and father on a little farm in the mountains, in France.

One day their father, Monsieur Dubonnet, received a letter from America.

"This is from your uncle," said Monsieur Dubonnet. "He wants you to come to America and visit your little cousins."

Gaston and Josephine clapped their hands and danced with joy.

"Oh, what fun! What fun!" they cried. Gaston and Josephine were very happy. They waved their handkerchiefs from the window.

"Bon voyage!" called Monsieur Dubonnet. But Madame Dubonnet's heart was sad.

"Oh, my!" she sighed. "America is a very far-off place. It will be a long time before they will come back to me."

The train had hardly left the station when Gaston and Josephine discovered that they were hungry. They went to the dining car and ordered all the good things on the menu.

When the train reached Paris the little pigs were very tired and went to a small hotel.

After a good night's sleep, Gaston was up and dressed early. But Josephine felt lazy and had her breakfast in bed.

They rode all through the streets of Paris in a big blue bus. Gaston and Josephine opened their eyes very wide. The bus crossed the bridge to the Place de la Concorde.

"What a lovely city!" said the two little pigs.

The trees on the Champs Elysées were so green in the bright sunshine. And there was the river Seine.

After lunch they went to the Jardin des Plantes. That is the name of the zoo in Paris. Josephine gave peanuts to a monkey who thanked her and said, "Au revoir, Mademoiselle."

The lion and the tiger did not like

peanuts. They would much rather have eaten the little rosy pigs themselves.

After a while, Gaston and Josephine felt hot and thirsty, so they decided to sit at the terrace of a little café near the zoo. But when the time came to pay the waiter for their orangeades, Gaston could not find his wallet.

"Oh my goodness!" cried Josephine. "All our money is gone and our steamship tickets, too!"

"Run, run. Maybe we can find it," said Gaston. They both jumped up and hurried back to the zoo. They heard someone call them. It was the monkey Josephine had fed with peanuts.

"Are you looking for your wallet?" he said. "The kangaroo found it. I saw her put it in her pocket."

Gaston and Josephine told the guard, who went into the kangaroo's cage and searched in her pocket—and there was a wallet!

"Yes, that's it!" cried Gaston and Josephine.

The kangaroo looked very much ashamed.

Now they could go to the opera. On the stage, they saw a handsome man and a pretty lady dressed in velvet. But it was hard to hear what they were saying—the music was so loud.

At last the time came to leave Paris. Gaston and Josephine with all their bags took a taxicab to go to the station.

They were a little late and very nearly missed the boat train.

The boat train didn't carry a dining car and the little pigs had forgotten to bring any lunch.

Poor Gaston was so hungry, he could not bear it any longer. He climbed up on the seat and pulled the alarm bell.

The train stopped. Gaston and Josephine opened the door and jumped out. A very angry conductor came after them.

"So you pulled that bell!" he said.

"Yes, sir. We thought we would get some milk from the cows in that field," said Gaston.

"Oh, you would, would you?" said the angry conductor. "All right, go ahead."

Josephine milked one of the cows. They took turns drinking out of Gaston's cap.

Then they ran about in the meadow. Gaston rolled in the grass. Josephine picked flowers for a bouquet. They had so much fun that they never saw the train go away without them.

It grew darker and darker. The little pigs were lost in the fields. What were they going to do?

"Oh, why did we get off the train?" said Josephine, sobbing in her handkerchief.

They walked and walked and at last came to a farmhouse. The farmer stood in the doorway, enjoying his pipe.

"Good evening, sir," said Gaston, and told him all that had happened.

"It's lucky you came here," said the farmer. "I am very fond of little pigs and I'll take good care of you."

The wicked farmer rubbed his hands with glee. He thought Gaston and Josephine looked nice and tender and would make a fine roast, and he shut them up in his pigpen.

"Oh dear, what ever will become of us?" cried poor Josephine. "Oh dear, oh dear, those pigs are so dirty! And they have such very bad manners!"

"Never mind, little sister," said Gaston, "we'll escape from this prison all right!"

It seemed they waited a long time for their chance. At last, late in the morning, they saw the mayor of the town going out to hunt with all his friends. Quickly Gaston and Josephine jumped out of the window.

The little pigs threw themselves at the mayor's feet.

"Save us, Mr. Mayor!" they cried. "We were on our way to America to visit our little cousins.

"And now that wicked man is going to eat us! Oh, save us! . . . Save us! . . ."

"Don't cry, little pigs," said the mayor. "I will help you. Here, take my bicycle and go to your boat. It will do me good to walk. I'm too fat anyway. I will punish this mean farmer as he deserves. Hurry along but be careful not to go too fast!"

Gaston and Josephine started out on the mayor's bicycle. Gaston pushed the pedals as hard as he could and tried to go

very fast so they would catch the boat.

"If only we don't have a flat tire," said Josephine.

At last they came to Havre. And there was the boat! It had not sailed! Gaston and Josephine rushed to the gangway and climbed on board.

As soon as the boat was out at sea it began to pitch and roll in the waves. Gaston and Josephine didn't feel very well. They decided it would be more comfortable to stay on deck instead of going down into the dining room.

For once they weren't hungry.

But when the sea was calm again they felt much better and played games way up on the top deck.

They rushed forward and climbed way up to the crow's nest.

They opened their mouths wide:

"Squeak! . . . Squeak! . . . Squeak! . . ."

What a good idea! The other ships heard the little pigs and kept out of the way. The captain was very proud of the two little French passengers and took care of them. He sent them hot milk to keep them from getting hoarse.

"Two more days and we'll be in New York," said Gaston.

Next morning a thick fog rolled in. Gaston and Josephine were very surprised. It seemed to come from nowhere. The horizon disappeared. . . .Then the sky. . . .Then even the water. . . .

They saw the captain running. He looked very worried.

"What's the matter, sir?" asked Gaston, running after him.

"The siren is out of order," said the captain. "And now other boats cannot hear us coming. This is a dreadful fog and goodness knows what will happen to us!"

It was a desperate situation. The passengers were afraid. The captain was very brave. He had once been shipwrecked on a desert island.

Gaston and Josephine had an idea.

After a while the fog lifted. Gaston and Josephine were heroes! They looked modest and even blushed a little but really they were very proud. All the passengers congratulated them.

"You are wonderful little pigs," said the captain. "Without you we all might have drowned."

And he invited them to have dinner at his table.

At last the boat arrived in New York. Reporters and many other important people came in tugs to meet Gaston and Josephine. They had heard all about them over the radio.

Their uncle and cousins were waiting on the pier. They, too, had heard how Gaston and Josephine saved the ship.

"Congratulations, congratulations!" they said as soon as Gaston and Josephine walked down the gangplank.

“Now we must take the train for three more days,” said their uncle, “before we get to our ranch in the West.”

“Oh, we don’t mind. We love to travel!” said Gaston and Josephine.

GOOD MORNING
and GOOD NIGHT

By JANE WERNER

Illustrated by ELOISE WILKIN

There was once a little boy who, strange as it may seem, did not like to get up in the morning—imagine that!

Every day his mother had to call him and call him to wake him, and each day it was harder than it had been the day before.

At last one morning he just would not wake up at all!

His mother called, "Time to get up, Sonny!"

But the little boy did not wake up.

His father called, "Time to roll out, Son!"

But the little boy did not wake up.

His sister and brother called, "Hurry up, lazy bones! We're almost ready for breakfast!"

But still that little boy slept on.

Then his kitten came and jumped on the little boy's head and mewed at him.

But that did not wake him.

His puppy bounced up and down on the little boy's tummy and licked his sleepy face with a quick, wet tongue.

But even that did not wake him.

The parrot from next door perched on his window sill and screeched at him.

And a black panther from the zoo came and snarled most horribly at him.

And a lion roared a great, tremendous roar that shook the walls.

But still that sleepy little boy slept on.

"Well, we've done all we could," said his mother with a sigh.

So they all went downstairs for breakfast.

Close by, while the hall seemed quite empty, out of a little mouse hole down at the floor popped a tiny gray mouse.

The little mouse sat in his doorway and wiggled his whiskers for a moment.

Then, when he was quite certain that everyone was eating breakfast, the little mouse scampered up to the little boy's

room, over to the bed, and up onto the little boy's pillow.

He put his pointed little nose very close to the little boy's ear and whispered, ever so softly, "Good morning!"

At that the sleepy little boy's eyes popped wide open.

"Good morning to you!" he said. "My, but I'm hungry!"

And he sprang out of bed, and washed and dressed in a flash, and ran down the stairs to breakfast. And the tiny little mouse went, too.

There was once a little girl who, strange as it may seem, did not like to go to bed—imagine that!

Every evening she wanted to stay up and play.

And every evening her mother said, "Bedtime, Sister! Hurry and get ready for bed!"

But every evening that little girl replied, "Oh, dear. I am wide awake. I still want to play."

So one evening her mother said, "Very well. You may stay up. But I am afraid you will have to play alone.

"Your brothers are going to sleep, and your daddy and I are going to sleep, so you will be all alone. Good night, my little wide-awake girl."

"Good night," said the little girl. "I do not mind being alone. I shall play with my toys."

First she went to her dollhouse.

But her dolls had been playing all day long, and now they were fast asleep.

"Well then," said the little girl to herself, "I will build with the blocks."

So she looked for the blocks, but they were all tucked away for the night.

"Oh," she said.

"Well, I will play with the Noah's ark."

But the Noah's ark was dark and silent.

All the animals two by two were fast asleep, and Mr. and Mrs. Noah were fast asleep, too.

"Well," said the little girl, "I will play with my sleepy doll. She sleeps all day so she must be wide awake at night."

But the sleepy doll was upstairs in the little girl's bedroom.

So the little girl crept very quietly up the stairs, past the room where her brothers were fast asleep, and past the room where her father and mother were fast asleep, and into her own little room.

There was the sleepy doll, safe and sound, but the sleepy doll was fast asleep, too.

And the whole house was so dark and quiet and full of sleep that the little girl's eyes began to feel very heavy.

So she took the sleepy doll in her arms and curled up in her own little bed, and soon that wide-awake little girl was fast asleep, too.

GUESS WHO LIVES HERE

By LOUISE WOODCOCK

Illustrated by ELOISE WILKIN

Somebody lives in this house.
He wears green overalls
And a striped sweater.
He likes to ride a bike
And build with blocks.
Guess who it is!
It's Terry.

Somebody else lives in this house.
She has curly hair and she smiles very often.
She wears a dress and sometimes an apron.
She cooks good things to eat every night,
And she tucks Terry into bed
with a kiss.
Guess who it is!
It's Terry's mother.
Somebody else lives in this house.
He is very tall,
And he walks with long steps.
He goes out to work in the morning
And sometimes he brings Terry a present
when he comes home at night.
Guess who it is!
It's Terry's father.
Somebody else lives in this house.
She is very short.
She can't stand up even holding onto
a chair.
She takes her milk out of a bottle.
She has only three teeth.
Guess who it is!
It's Terry's baby sister.
Somebody else lives in this house.
He has rough brown hair and a tail
he can wag.
All he can say is "Bow-wow!" or "Woof-woof!"
He loves to go everywhere Terry goes.
Guess who it is!
It's Terry's dog Wolfie.
Somebody else lives in this house.
She is soft and furry.
She has claws that can scratch but she
doesn't scratch very often.
She drinks milk from a saucer on the floor.
She likes to sleep in nice warm places.
Guess who it is!
It's Terry's cat Silkie.
Somebody else lives in this house.
He is very very tiny
And can run very fast.
He is gray all over and his tail's like a
little sharp spike.
He only comes out at night to hunt for
crumbs.
Guess who it is!
It's the mouse in Terry's cellar.

Somebody lives in the big tree beside this house.
She lives in a nest that she built on a branch.
She has four blue eggs in that nest.
She sits on the nest to keep the eggs warm,
Because her babies are inside them.
Guess who it is!
It's a mother robin.
Somebody else lives in the tree by this house.
He has long gray fur
And a beautiful wavy tail.
He can jump very far from one branch to another.
He loves to eat nuts in his tiny sharp claws.
Guess who it is!
It's a squirrel.
Sometimes somebody comes to this house before anyone in it is awake.
He doesn't ring the doorbell.
He sets down some bottles on the porch.
He picks up the empty bottles Terry's mother has put there.
Then he goes on to the house next door.
Guess who it is!
It's the milkman on Terry's street.
Sometimes somebody rings the doorbell of this house.
He wears a blue suit.
He carries a big heavy bag on his back.
He takes letters out of his bag,
And puts them in the box beside the front door.
Guess who it is!
It's the postman on Terry's street

Some days something comes down from the sky—
"Patter-pit-patter!" it says on the roof.
"Splashity-splash!" it says on the walk.
The flowers in the window box shine with wetness,
And all the leaves on the big tree drip.
Guess what it is!
It's the rain.
But most days there's something shining down on this house.
It makes the flowers in the window box grow.
It makes all the people say to each other,
"What a very nice day it is today!"
Guess what it is!
It's the sunshine.
Sometimes something blows round and round this house.

It says "Whoo-oo!" in the chimney.
It rattles the windows.
It swings the nest on the branch of the tree.
Guess what it is!
It's the wind.
Sometimes at night something shines on this house.
It isn't warm like the sun.
Sometimes it's a thin little silver curve.
Sometimes it looks like half of a cookie.
Sometimes it's big and round and shines like a mirror.
It shines on the squirrel in his little tree house.
It shines on the robin in her nest on the branch.
It shines on Terry's father and mother fast asleep.
It shines in the window at the mouse on the floor—
And at Silkie too sleepy to chase him.
It shines on Terry—
And on Wolfie stretched out on the floor.
Guess what it is!
It's the moon!

THE SEVEN SNEEZES

By OLGA CABRAL

Illustrated by TIBOR GERGELY

There were once a bunny, a kitten, and a dog who lived together in a back yard.

The bunny was white, with long, fluffy ears.

The kitten was black, and like all kittens it had teeny ears.

The dog was a great big dog with a great big bark.

Everybody was happy, everybody was satisfied. The bunny loved his big ears, the kitten was glad that hers were tiny, and the dog was proud of his great big bark.

One day a rag man came along in an old wagon. "Any rags today? Any rags today?" sang the man.

It was a chilly day. The rag man started to sneeze—

"Any r—ah—ah—ah—ah—"

The bunny, the kitten, and the dog all held their breath until the rag man finished his sneeze—

"A—choo! A—cha! A—chachoo!"

They were three hearty sneezes. So hearty, that the rag man was blown out of sight down the road—wagon and horse and all!

"Goodness gracious—" the bunny, the kitten, and the dog started to say to each other. And then they saw something strange had happened to them!

The black kitten had the bunny's long, white ears.

The white bunny had the kitten's teeny black ears.

"Why, how silly you both look!" said the dog.

The next minute, he felt silly. Because, when he opened his mouth no great big bark came out. Instead, his voice was only a teeny weeny little meow.

Things were certainly mixed up!

The bunny felt his short, teeny ears. He squeaked.

The kitten, felt her long, overgrown ears.

"Goodness gracious me!" she said.

But she said it in a terrible, great big bark! And she fell over backward, so surprised was she to hear herself barking.

Then the kitten saw her teeny ears on the bunny's head. "Give me back my ears!" she said.

She ran over to the bunny and tried to pull them off.

The bunny saw his long ears on the kitten's head.

"Give me back my ears!" he said.

He tried to pull them off too.

And the dog ran around them, meowing like a cat.

"Oh dear!" barked the cat. "What happened to us?"

"Everything was fine," meowed the dog, "until the rag man came."

The bunny had hiccups, he was so upset.

"The—sneezes—did—it!" he said between hiccups.

They brought him a drink of water.

"Now what are we going to do?" said the dog in his baby-kitten voice.

They thought and thought and then the bunny said, "We must find the rag man."

"And make him put everything back the way it was," said the dog. "If he can!"

So they set out to find the rag man.

Soon they met a goose without any feathers. She was carrying all her feathers in a little basket.

"Pardon us," said the bunny, the cat, and the dog, "but did you see a rag man go by this way?"

"Can't you see that he did?" asked the goose, angrily stamping her foot. "He sneezed off all my feathers! And I'm going to find him and make him put them back on again—if he can!"

So they all went along together.

Pretty soon they met a rooster carrying his comb in his beak. His tail feathers grew on top of his head.

"Pardon us," said the bunny, the cat, the dog, and the pink goose, "but did you see—"

"That awful rag man!" said the rooster angrily. "It's wicked to go around sneezing folk's combs off! I'm going to make him put it back again—if he can!"

So they all went along together.

And pretty soon they met a little girl standing in the road, curling her toes and crying over two long braids that had been sneezed right off her head!

So she and the animals all went along together.

Pretty soon they met a little boy, who looked strange because he was wearing only half a jacket, and only one shoe. He held the other half of his jacket, and the other shoe was stuck very tightly upside down on his head.

"So you've been sneezed at too?" the little boy said to the animals and the little girl. "Let's find that rag man," he said, "and make him fix us up—if he can!"

So they all went along together, and walked and walked until they came to a tumble-down house with an old horse and wagon standing in front. And inside the house someone sneezed **"Kerchaya!"**

The sneeze blew the horse and wagon up into the air. They came down again on the roof of the tumble-down house.

"This is the right place all right!" said the little boy. So the funny animals and the strange little boy and girl ran into the rag man's house and crowded around him.

"What will my mother say when I tell her I've lost my pigtails?" cried the little girl.

"They'll laugh at me in school with a shoe on my head!" cried the little boy.

"No one will love me with these little ears!" squeaked the bunny.

"Or me with these big ears!" barked the cat.

"How can I guard the house without my great big bark?" meowed the dog.

"I'll freeze without my feathers!" cried the goose.

"No barnyard will have me!" cried the rooster.

"Please don't be angry, my dears," said the rag man. "I guess my sneezes must be magic. I will do my best to sneeze everything right again."

So the rag man sat down to sneeze a magic sneeze.

"Just sprinkle a little pepper on my nose to help," he said.

So the little girl poured a BIG swish of pepper on the rag man's nose, and suddenly—**"Choo! Buttonmyshoe! Switcheroo!"** the rag man sneezed.

The furniture flew out of the window! The house lifted into the air! So did the horse and wagon. So did the fence. And they all came down with a bang in an utterly different place, a much nicer place than before.

"More pepper!" gasped the rag man. The little girl threw the can of pepper at him. Then—

"Katchoo!" The bunny's ears and

the kitten's ears flew into the air and came down in their right places!

"Katchim!" The dog jumped up and barked!

"Katcham!" The kitten mewed.

"Kutchibble!" The feathers in the little basket flew onto the goose again!

"Fiddle-Faddle!" The little girl's pigtails were back on her head.

"Skedaddle!" The little boy's jacket and shoes were where they should be!

"Fumadiddle!" The rooster's comb flew onto his head and his tail feathers stuck where tail feathers should grow!

Everything was back the way it was!

Then suddenly the rag man looked sneezy again.

"Run," he cried. "Run while I hold my nose!"

So everyone ran!

And before the rag man could sneeze again, they had run all the way home.

Johnny's MACHINES

By HELEN PALMER

Illustrated by CORNELIUS DEWITT

"Grandfather," said Johnny, "I like to push buttons . . . buttons that make things work. I like to push the button that flashes on the light, and the one that starts the radio. We ought to have more buttons here on the farm . . . more buttons to make more things work."

"We do need more things like that," said Johnny's grandfather. "I'll drive to the village and bring home some new machines in my car."

Johnny's grandfather drove to the village and came back with his car piled high with new machines . . . little machines and big machines, all wrapped up in brown paper, tied with red string. Johnny could hardly wait to tear off the paper and find out what was inside.

"Now Johnny," said his grandfather, "you may push the buttons. Make all the new machines work."

Johnny made the new TOASTER toast. He saw the toasted toast pop right up into the air.

He made the new MIXER mix. It mixed up a caramel frosting for his grandfather's birthday cake.

He made the new FREEZER freeze a big dish of strawberry ice cream.

He made the new SEWING MACHINE sew. It stitched up a new pair of sails for his boat.

"And here's a machine," said Johnny's grandfather, "for making your sailboat sail." He led Johnny into the kitchen.

He pushed a button. Whrr! An electric fan whirled round!

What a wind! Johnny floated his boat in the tub. Whee! It raced along. The spray flew fast.

In the bedroom, Johnny pushed another button. It turned on a big sun lamp. He put on his big, round sun goggles. It was just like a summer day at the beach.

"This is fun!" cried Johnny. "I like it! I'd like to push *more* new buttons to make more things work."

"Why, the house is just full of new buttons," said Johnny's grandfather. "Now you should be happy. We surely have enough."

"Not nearly enough," said Johnny. "We've made things work *inside* the house. Now I want to make things work *outdoors* on the farm."

Johnny's grandfather thought for a minute. Then he put on his hat and his coat and he went to the city. When he came back, he was riding in a truck piled high with new machines for the farm . . . enormous machines, tied on to the truck with thick rope.

Johnny helped to untie them.

First they untied a shiny new TRACTOR.

Johnny looked it all over. "Mmmm," he said. "What a funny kind of car . . . no top, no door, no windows! It's nothing but an engine on wheels. What's it for?"

"A tractor pulls things," said Johnny's grandfather. "It's just like a horse, but it's stronger. It can pull all sorts of things. It all depends on what you hitch on behind it."

"Let's hitch on a big new machine!" cried Johnny. "Then I'll push the buttons and make it work."

"Very well," said Johnny's grandfather. "We'll hitch on the PLOW. We'll make it dig up a field for planting."

They lifted the new plow down from the truck and hitched it to the tractor. Then up they climbed into the driver's seat. Johnny pushed a button. Pfftt! Brrr! They chugged off, with the plow bumping along behind them.

The plow had two sharp blades. They dug down into the hard earth, making it soft and fine . . . fine enough for planting.

"Now," said Johnny's grandfather, "we'll plant some oats. We'll do it with another machine . . . the SEEDER."

They unhitched the plow from the tractor and hitched on the seeder. Johnny pushed a button. Whee! Out into the air flew a great cloud of oats! They dropped to the ground like snowflakes, down into the soft earth the plow had dug up.

"Golly . . . I like this oats machine!" cried Johnny. "I wish we had more machines for the farm!"

"We have," said Johnny's grandfather. "Three more new ones! They're already in the barn!"

Down from the seeder! Off to the barn!

They pushed open the big red barn door and went in.

"First, look at this very tiny new machine," said Johnny's grandfather. "Looks like a toy . . . but it isn't. It's a SHEARER. It clips the wool from a sheep." He handed Johnny a small electric clipper. Then he brought him a white woolly sheep.

Johnny ran the shearer over the sheep. The wool came off just like a coat. He clipped all the wool from the white sheep, and then he clipped a black sheep too. "This is fun!" he cried. "I like it!"

"Here's something you'll like even better," said Johnny's grandfather. He led Johnny off to the corner of the barn where the ducks slept. "Come . . . push *this* button!"

Johnny did. It turned on a light inside a mysterious, round tin box. A crowd of tiny, quacking ducks came rushing toward the warm, bright light.

"But what is it?" cried Johnny.

wish the farm were ten times bigger!"

Johnny's grandfather smiled. "I knew you'd want to make it bigger, Johnny, so I sent for a great machine that *will* make it bigger. Listen, I hear it coming now!"

Something was chugging. Something was thumping . . . bump! bump! bump! just outside the barn.

"A BROODER," said Johnny's grandfather. "It's a heating machine for keeping the baby ducks warm."

Johnny watched the little ducks cuddling up inside the brooder. Then his eye caught sight of something else. "Ooo! Look!" He couldn't believe it, but there it was.

A MACHINE WAS MILKING A COW! It milked the milk right into a hose that poured it into a tall, glass jar.

"Jimminy!" cried Johnny. "*What* a machine! Now I wish we had *more* cows . . . *more* sheep . . . *more* ducks . . . I

They rushed outside and saw an enormous STEAM SHOVEL driving toward them.

"Wow!" cried Johnny. "It's as tall as a house. It's a shovel for a giant! What's it going to do?"

"It's going to make the farm bigger," said Johnny's grandfather. "It's going to cut down the hill to make a bigger field for the cows. Come now . . . climb aboard it! Push all the buttons that make the shovel work!"

The driver of the shovel helped Johnny to climb on.

"Get ready now," he said. "Push *this* button . . . push *that* button . . . now *this* one . . . now *that* one!"

G-r-r-r-mp! . . . g-r-r-r-nk! Chains clanked. The shovel scooped into the hill. It scooped up a great mouthful of earth and dumped it down into the hollow below. G-r-r-r-mp! . . . g-r-r-r-nk! It scooped up another mouthful.

"Jeepers!" cried Johnny. "It'll scoop up the whole hill in just a few bites."

It scooped again and again and again. Soon the hill was all flattened out.

"Great!" said Johnny. "Now the hill is gone, but the ground is still very bumpy. The cows won't like it. We'll have to smooth it out."

"You're right," said Johnny's grandfather. "A BULLDOZER is the machine to smooth it out. We'll get one right away."

The bulldozer was the most fun of all. It wasn't tall like the shovel. It was low and very wide. But the bulldozer did everything!

It squashed down bumps. It shaved down humps. It cut down all the old tree stumps the shovel had left behind!

It pushed away everything that got in the way. The rough, bumpy ground was soon a nice, smooth field where cows could walk about and have a very pleasant time.

"Grandfather!" shouted Johnny suddenly. "There's something else we ought to do! The duck pond! We ought to make it larger!"

"Maybe you're right, Johnny, but to do that, we must get the most enormous machine of all . . . a DREDGE!"

The dredge was so enormous it took two whole days to get there.

"Jimminy jeepers creepers!" Johnny had never seen anything like that dredge. "Why . . . why . . . it's a sort of dipper . . . a giant's dipper! That's what it is!" The next thing Johnny knew he was climbing aboard it. He pushed a button . . . Splash!

The dredge dipped down into the duck pond. Down, straight down to the very bottom! Glugg . . . glugg! Johnny heard it slicing through the muck.

He pushed another button. Clank! Up came the dredge dripping with a great dipperful of mud. It dumped the mud down beside the pond. Then down into the water it sloshed again. Then up again with another dipperful!

Hour after hour the dredge dug up the duck pond. Soon it was wide and deep like a lake.

"At last!" cried Johnny. "The farm is bigger! The field is five times bigger. The pond is ten times bigger. Now we can have twenty times more sheep, fifty times more cows, and hundreds and hundreds of fat white ducks!"

"Very well," said Johnny's grandfather, "we will."

And so they did. Johnny's grandfather felt very proud of Johnny.

"It was Johnny who made all these nice things happen," he said. "It was all because Johnny likes to push buttons . . . buttons that make things work."

LITTLE Yip-Yip AND HIS BARK

By KATHRYN *and* BYRON JACKSON

Illustrated by TIBOR GERGELY

One morning, a very small puppy woke up in a brand-new doghouse.

He sniffed at the cozy, dark inside . . . and he licked at the bright blue outside.

Then he blinked his eyes and looked all around the big busy barnyard.

"It's a wonderful place," he said to himself, "but oh, my, isn't it big?"

Just as he said that, all the big barnyard animals came running up to him.

"Are you the new watchdog?" asked the ducks. The little puppy liked that watchdog idea. He smiled and wagged his tail.

"I guess I am!" he said.

"Well then," crowed the big rooster, "let's hear your big watchdog bark!"

The puppy stood up tall and opened his mouth.

He took a deep breath.

And he barked, "Yip-yip-yip!"

The rooster turned to the pigs. "Did you hear anything?" he asked.

"We heard *something*," squealed the pigs. "It sounded like a squeaky shoe!"

And the calf said she thought it sounded like a baby robin calling its mother.

All the animals laughed and ran away very busily, and the puppy went into his new house. "Maybe my barking isn't all it should be," he said, and he ran out in the sunshine to practice.

But before he had time for one yip, a great big black dog came bounding up.

That big dog tasted the puppy's milk, and he nibbled the puppy's biscuit.

"Puppy food!" he snorted. "I'll come back when you have some real food for me to eat up!"

And he walked away with his head in the air.

The little puppy felt so cross that he barked until that big dog was out of sight.

"Yip-yip-yip!" he barked.

A little field mouse, on its way to the corn crib, heard that little bark. It jumped when it heard the first yip, but when it heard the second and third it sat down and laughed until tears dripped off its whiskers.

"Oh, ho, ho!" laughed the mouse. "I have baby mice at home who can bark louder than that!"

"Is that so!" cried the puppy. He ran at the mouse with all his sharp little teeth showing.

"I'll bite—"

But the mouse was gone! It had disappeared through the cracks in the corn crib, and the puppy was chasing nobody at all.

"Well," he barked proudly, "I guess I scared *him* all right!"

And then he heard all the mice in the corn crib barking little tiny barks.

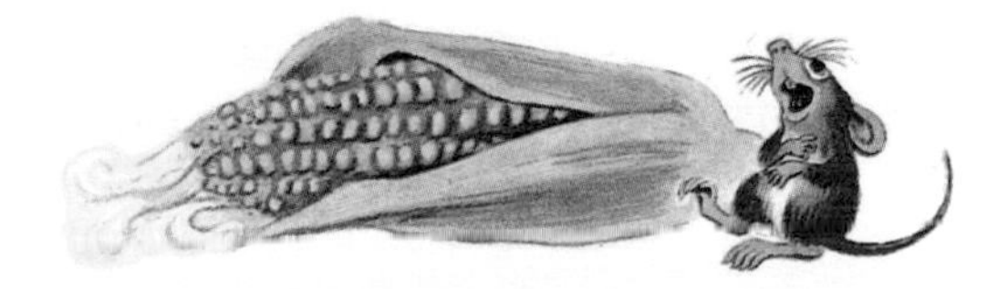

"Yip-yip-yip," they laughed. "Yip-yip! Oh, what a watchdog!"

He looked for something bigger to scare.

And just as it was getting dark he saw something *much* bigger.

A slim, sly, red fox came creeping into the barnyard.

He slithered straight toward the hen house, and he looked so mean and hungry that the little puppy backed away from him.

"I'll have to bark louder than ever this time," he whispered bravely, and he backed right into an empty milk pail. "You have to bark very loud to scare a fox."

The sly fox crept nearer and nearer and nearer to the hen house, licking his chops and snickering to himself. And then, all at once, the puppy took a deep breath and barked.

When that little bark came out of the milk pail, it wasn't a little yip-yip-yip at all! It echoed and rumbled around in the pail, and when it came out, it was a fine big bark.

It went: BOW-WOW-WOW! and it was so loud that the puppy jumped in the air, pail and all.

"Help!" squeaked the fox. He turned head over heels, and away he ran as fast as he could go.

The puppy picked himself up and barked a little yip-yip.

He ran back into the pail and barked a big BOW-WOW.

"Now I know how to scare the wits out of anything!" he cried. "All I have to do is hide in an empty something before I bark!"

And he trotted back to his brand-new house with his little tail wagging so fast that it looked like a pinwheel.

Early the next morning, a family of very hungry rabbits hopped into the farm garden.

They chewed tunnels in the biggest cabbages, and hopped through the tunnels. They bit big holes in the middle-sized cabbages, and little holes in the tiny little cabbages.

"Rabbits in the cabbage patch!" the rooster crowed. "Spoiling the whole cabbage patch!"

The little puppy woke up with a start. He ran across the barnyard and into the garden, barking his little yip-yip-yip.

And the rabbits stopped eating just long enough to swallow what they had in their mouths.

Then they jumped up and down on a row of young cabbages, laughing at that sleepy little bark.

"Oh, bad!" yipped the puppy. He started toward his milk pail. And then he said, "Oh, good!" and scampered into an empty barrel that was lying at the edge of the cabbage patch.

"Now for my best rabbit-scaring bark!" thought the little puppy. He closed his eyes and puffed out his chest and barked as loudly as he could.

The big, echoey barrel rolled the sound out, big and loud, into the garden.

BOW WOW
WOW WOW
WOW WOW!!

It came out such a big BOW-WOW-WOW that the rabbits' ears stood on end.

"Watchdogs!" they cried. "At least four great big ones!"

They hopped lickety-split out of the cabbage patch and over the fence. In one second there wasn't a rabbit to be seen!

"That was even better than the milk pail!" laughed the little puppy.

Then he thought he might find something still louder. He nosed all around the farm, barking in every empty thing he found.

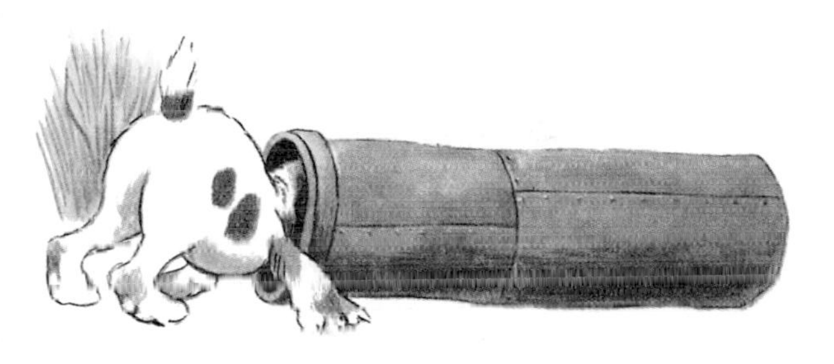

He barked in a rusty milk can.

And he barked in a big round pipe.

And then one day he found an old oil drum.

He ran in that and barked, "Where's that big black dog now?"

And his bark sounded like this:

BOW WOW
WOW WOW
WOW WOW!!

The puppy liked that oil-drum bark. He practiced it every day—and every day his own little bark grew bigger and bigger. But he never noticed that.

The farmer didn't like all this noise.

"You're a fine watchdog, little puppy," he said. "But you'll have to use your own little bark after tomorrow, because I'm going to clean up the farm."

The next day while the farmer worked, the puppy ran at his heels.

"Oh, don't take my barrel!" he barked.

And he barked,"Don't take my oil drum!"

And then he barked, "Don't take my milk can—or that old pipe. Oh, I need those old pails!"

But into the junk wagon they went.

"All my barking things are gone," cried the little puppy. "Now, what will I do when that big black dog comes back?"

And the very minute he said that, along came the big black dog! He walked boldly through the puppy's barnyard. He walked right up to the little puppy's house.

He licked up all the puppy's milk, and *then* he picked up the puppy's new chewing bone.

That was too much for the little puppy.

He ran at the big black dog like a small thunderbolt.

He was so angry that he barked for all he was worth, and by this time his own bark was a real big

BOW WOW WOW!

It was even bigger than his oil-drum bark!

The big dog never stopped to see how big the little puppy was. He just dropped that bone and ran, with the puppy snapping at his tail. He jumped over the fence, he raced down the road, and he *never* came back.

Everybody on the farm came running out to see that chase.

"Just look at our watchdog!" squealed the pigs.

"And just listen to his bark!" the rooster crowed.

The farmer's wife was so pleased that she ran into the house for an old soft pillow. She put it in the doghouse.

"It will make a nice bed for our watchdog," she said.

The farmer filled the puppy's bowl with cream. He brought out a little dish of gravy with some fine juicy scraps of meat in it. He put a new chewing bone full of tidbits beside the old chewing bone. And then he whistled a long, loud whistle for the little puppy.

When the little puppy got back to his house, he was the most surprised puppy in the whole world.

First, he barked a good-sized bark to say "Thank you," and then he began to eat. He ate until his little sides were as round as a pumpkin.

He tried out his lovely new bed.

It was so soft and comfortable that he almost fell asleep.

But he had one more thing to do.

The little puppy stood up on his four little feet and wagged his tail.

And just to make sure he was really a real watchdog at last, he barked the loudest kind of bark—

BOW
WOW
WOW

THE COLOR KITTENS

By MARGARET WISE BROWN

Illustrated by ALICE *and* MARTIN PROVENSEN

Once there were two color kittens with green eyes, Brush and Hush. They liked to mix and make colors by splashing one color into another. They had buckets and buckets and buckets and buckets of color to splash around with. Out of these colors they would make all the colors in the world.

The buckets had the colors written on them, but of course the kittens couldn't read. They had to tell by the colors. "It is very easy," said Brush.

"Red is red. Blue is blue," said Hush.

But they had no green. "No green paint!" said Brush and Hush. And they wanted green paint, of course, because nearly every place they liked to go was green.

Green as cats' eyes
Green as grass
By streams of water
Green as glass.

So they tried to make some green paint.

Brush mixed red paint and white paint together—and what did that make? It didn't make green.

But it made pink.
Pink as pigs
Pink as toes
Pink as a rose
Or a baby's nose.

Then Hush mixed yellow
and red together, and it made orange.
Orange as an orange tree
Orange as a bumblebee
Orange as the setting sun
Sinking slowly in the sea.

The kittens were delighted, but it didn't make green.

Then they mixed red and blue together—and what did that make? It didn't make green. It made a deep dark purple.

Purple as violets
Purple as prunes
Purple as shadows on late afternoons.

Still no green. And then . . .

O wonderful kittens! O Brush! O Hush!

At last, almost by accident, the kittens poured a bucket of blue and a bucket of yellow together, and it came to pass that they made a green as green as grass.

Green as green leaves on a tree
Green as islands in the sea.

The little kittens were so happy with all the colors they had made that they began to paint everything around them. They painted . . .

Green leaves
and red berries
and purple flowers
and pink cherries
Red tables and yellow chairs
Black trees with golden pears.

Then the kittens got so excited they knocked their buckets upside down and all the colors ran together. Yellow, red, a little blue and a little black . . . and that made brown.

Brown as a tugboat
Brown as an old goat
Brown as a beaver

BROWN

And in all that brown, the sun went down. It was evening and the colors began to disappear in the warm dark night.

The kittens fell asleep in the warm dark night with all their colors out of sight and as they slept they dreamed their dream—

A wonderful dream
Of a red rose tree
That turned all white
When you counted three
One . . . Two . . . Three

Of a purple land
In a pale pink sea
Where apples fell
From a golden tree
And then a world of Easter eggs
That danced about on little short legs.

And they dreamed
Of a mouse
A little gray mouse
That danced on a cheese
That was big as a house
And a green cat danced
With a little pink dog
Till they all disappeared in a soft gray fog.

And suddenly Brush woke up and Hush woke up. It was morning. They crawled out of bed into a big bright world. The sky was wild with sunshine.

The kittens were wild
with purring
and pouncing—

They got so pouncy they knocked over the buckets and all the colors ran out together.

There were all the colors in the world and the color kittens had made them.

I CAN FLY

By RUTH KRAUSS

Illustrated by MARY BLAIR

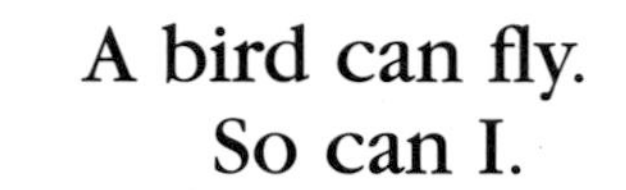

A bird can fly.
So can I.

A cow can moo.

I can too.

Who can walk like a bug? Me! Ug ug.

I'm merrier than a terrier.

Swish! I'm a fish.

Pick pick pick I'm a little chick.

Who can live in a hole? Me! Like a mole.

Who can climb anywhere? Me! Like a bear.

My house is like a mouse's.

A clam is what I am.

Pop pop pop I'm a rabbit with a hop.

Bump bump bump I'm a camel with a hump.

Haw haw haw

I'm a donkey in the straw.

Pitter pitter pat

I can walk like a cat.

Howl howl howl I'm an old screech owl.

Gubble gubble gubble
I'm a mubble in a pubble.
I can play
I'm anything that's anything.
That's MY way.

THE LITTLE FAT POLICEMAN

By MARGARET WISE BROWN
and EDITH THACHER HURD
Illustrated by ALICE *and* MARTIN PROVENSEN

STOP AND GO

The Little Fat Policeman stood in the middle of the street. He wore a new blue uniform with shiny buttons down the front. On his chest a silver badge said:

The Little Fat Policeman directed all the whizzing traffic. He wore white gloves so that everyone could see his hands wave. And he blew a silver whistle.

Everybody knew the Little Fat Policeman. When he blew his whistle the cars and trucks all stopped, until he waved his hand again for all the cars to go.

One day a lady with a bouncing baby in a carriage and six little funny-faced children wanted to cross the street.

The Little Fat Policeman blew his whistle extra hard and put up both his hands.

EVERYBODY STOP!......

Then he wheeled the bouncing baby safe across the street.

The lady thanked him. He saluted smartly. And all the funny-faced children smiled.

And he returned to his traffic, and there he stood.

Up came a red truck— STOP
Up came a blue car— STOP
Up came a yellow car— STOP
Up came a pink car
and blew its horn— STOP
Up came a green car— STOP
Up came three jeeps— STOP
Up came a flower wagon— STOP
Up came a moving van— STOP
Up came a motorcycle— STOP
Up came a bicycle— STOP

Then the Little Fat Policeman gave them a look, raised his silver whistle to his mouth, and blew

GO!......

Brr-rr went the red truck,
Brr-rr went the blue car,
Brr-rr went the yellow car,
Whump went the pink car,
Brr-rr went the green car,
Brr-rr-rr went the three jeeps,
Giddy ap! went the flower wagon,
Brr-rr went the moving van,
Brr-rr went the motorcycle,
and Whee went the bicycle.

GONE!......

The road was empty except for the Little Fat Policeman, who took off his hat and scratched his head.

Then way down the road he saw something coming fast—too fast. Zip—it grew bigger and bigger.

The Little Fat Policeman blew his whistle three times and waved his arms.

The car stopped and a lady leaned out and said, "Oh, dear! Oh, dear!"

"Too fast, lady!" said the Little Fat Policeman. "Why were you going so fast?"

"I was singing a very fast song and I forgot," said the lady. "I am very sorry."

"What were you singing?" asked the Little Fat Policeman.

"Glow, Little Glow Worm, Glimmer, Glimmer."

"Sing a slow song next time," said the Little Fat Policeman, "and don't forget or I'll have to give you a ticket and send you up before a judge."

Then he blew his whistle and waved her along. "Sing *Oh What a Beautiful Morning* next time," he called. And he started to hum it himself. Then down the road came—believe it or not—elephants, tigers in cages, clowns, monkeys, ladies on white horses, bears and peanuts.

The Circus had come to town.

So the Little Fat Policeman stopped all the cars at the crossroads and slowly but surely the circus went down the street.

A big parade!

With lions and tigers and a noisy brass band.

THE SUDDEN TELEPHONE CALL

But the Little Fat Policeman wasn't always just a traffic cop. Sometimes he waited in his Police Booth for exciting things to happen. One day a nice old lady called.

"Policeman, please!" said she. "I'm a Policeman," said he.

"Come quick as you can," said she. "My cat is up in the top of a tree and won't come down to me."

"I'll be right there," said he. "Just sit in your chair and I'll be right there."

The Little Fat Policeman put on his goggles, jumped on his red motorcycle, and stepped on the gas. He whizzed away.

"Oh, Little Fat Policeman, you've come just in time."

The old lady wrung her hands.

She mopped her eyes and began to jump about as if she had a fire inside her boots.

The Little Fat Policeman looked around but he couldn't see the cat until the old lady pointed to the top of a prickly pear tree—and THERE on top sat a cat!

The Little Fat Policeman didn't like to climb up prickly pear trees. He knew he was too fat, and he knew prickly pears were prickly. So he called the fire house.

The hook and ladder arrived in a jiffy. The firemen put a ladder up to the cat. And a fireman climbed up and brought the old lady's cat almost down, when—lickety split—the cat jumped out of his arms.

But the Little Fat Policeman jumped, as quick as lighting, after the cat.

He caught the cat in both his hands and gave it to the nice old lady. She hugged the cat and then she hugged the Little Fat Policeman. The cat was pushed between them. Meow!

THE BURGLAR IN THE DARK

One dark night the Little Fat Policeman was waiting quietly at the Police Booth. He was all alone.

Br-rr-rr rang the telephone. Someone said, "Come fast, I think I hear a burglar prowling in my house."

The Little Fat Policeman stuck his pistol in his holster. He grabbed his stout policeman's billy.

Whee-ee-ee went the siren on the policeman's little car.

Then he turned the siren off and crept silently through the night. One Little Fat Policeman!

He crept up to the house. He walked on tiptoes, creeping, creeping. He flashed his flashlight all around.

He looked in the bushes and he looked in the trees.

He patted the pistol in the holster at his side. It was there, all right. He flashed his flashlight.

But there was no burglar there.

He went in the house. He crept in the hall.

Creeping, creeping, he flashed his flashlight.

But there was no burglar there.

There was just a tiny little noise—a sort of scratching sound!

The Little Fat Policeman grabbed his pistol in his hand.

"Who's there?" he shouted softly.

The scratching stopped.

Instead there was a GROAN! and a SNEEZE!

The Little Fat Policeman pointed his pistol at the groan and the sneeze. Then he flashed his flashlight—FLASH!

And suddenly there was a lot of scrambling and a barking and a whining for joy.

Because that dreadful burglar was only a—BIG WOOLLY SHEEP DOG who had lost his way.

The Little Fat Policeman laughed a big fat belly laugh, a great big warm laugh. Then he patted the woolly sheep dog, who wagged his tail and licked the Little Fat Policeman's hand.

The Little Fat Policeman put him in his car and drove him home to the right house because he knew the boy who owned him.

THE BRAVE LIFE SAVER

Every Sunday morning the Little Fat Policeman took it easy. His wife shined his badge.

He liked to smoke his pipe and read his paper and go for a walk with his wife.

One Sunday the sun was shining brightly.

The birds were singing sweetly.

The Little Fat Policeman and his wife walked beside the ocean on the yellow sand. There were people lying on the beach. There were people swimming in the green sea. The Little Fat Policeman was eating a peach, when suddenly there was a dreadful yell:

"Help! Help! Help!"

The Little Fat Policeman saw a man who couldn't swim rolling in the waves.

As quick as a wink, before the man could sink, the Little Fat Policeman threw off his blue coat, kicked off his boots, threw down his cap, and ran. Down the beach he ran and took a dive into the waves.

And he dove and swam and kicked and splashed through the great, green, curling ocean.

The man kept bobbing up and down ahead of him and floating out to sea.

The Little Fat Policeman had learned how to rescue people when he went to policeman's school, so he knew what to do. He grabbed the man by the top of his head.

He pulled him by the hair, and swam with him up great, green waves, like mountains in the sea, until he swam safe back to shore.

The Little Fat Policeman's wife danced with joy. She danced upon the yellow sand. And all the people from the beach made a tremendous crowd. They shouted three hurrahs:

"Hurrah!
  Hurrah!
    Hurrah!
      For the Little Fat Policeman
      The finest cop of all!"

And a little boy sang:

"Yo-ho-ho
Yes-sir-ree
O Policeman,
Please save me."

2. One Policeman all alone
   In his round house
   With his phone.
   Ting-ling-ling
   Rings in his ear—
   This Policeman's always near.
      Yo ho ho!
      Yes siree!
      O Policeman,
      Please save me.

3. One Policeman on the beach
   Keeps his feet dry,
   Eats his peach.
   Help! Help! Help!
   Now don't you fear—
   This Policeman's always near.
      Yo ho ho!
      Yes siree!
      O Policeman,
      Please save me.

BRAVE COWBOY BILL

By KATHRYN *and* BYRON JACKSON

Illustrated by RICHARD SCARRY

Of all the hands on Bar H ranch, the bravest was brave Cowboy Bill. He wore tight boots with heels THAT high, a ten-gallon hat that hid one eye, and sheepskin chaps with flaps.

He named his pony Golden Arrow.

And every day with a clip and a clop, he rode to the highest mountain top.

One day he saw some bad men who were stealing Bar H cattle!

Then he tightened up his stirrups, so they wouldn't clink or rattle—and rode, with both guns ready, to the valley where they were.

"Stick 'em up!" he shouted loudly, and he added, "Don't you stir!"

All the bad men put their hands up. And they all stood very still.

Because NO one ever argued with the daring Cowboy Bill.

Next he took those desperate outlaws at a gallop, side by side, all across the rolling prairie. 'Twas a most exciting ride to the office of the sheriff (who was twice as pleased as punch).

Then Bill rounded up wild horses until almost time for lunch.

Lunch was buffalo or deer meat, that he shot himself and cooked on a fire made out of brushwood.

"Now," he said, "it's time for roundup!"

But before he'd quite begun, all the cattle put their ears down, and they all began to run.

And they snorted.

And they bellowed.

And they wouldn't hear or heed. And they ran all helter-skelter. They were trying to stampede.

Cowboy Bill just rode around them, shouting "Yip-py ai ki ay!" till he chased them in a valley where they couldn't get away.

Then he built a fire for branding.

And he branded and he branded till his calves were all marked Bar H—and he did it single-handed!

When a puma cat came prowling, hungry for a Bar H calf—or a grizzly bear came growling—you could hear that cowboy laugh just before he pulled his trigger.

BANG! BANG! BANG! He shot it dead.

Then he skinned it for a blanket or a pillow for his head. (Though he wasn't one for sleeping.)

Cowboy Bill sat up all night, singing songs about his cattle, near his campfire big and bright.

And at dawn he drove them slowly 'cross the prairie—into town—to the railroad, where he sold them with a busy kind of frown, for a lot of golden dollars, to some big men from the East.

Then he bought new boots and bullets.

And he had a splendid feast in the town's most splendid restaurant. He had lamb chops and new peas.

And some homemade cornbread, buttered,
Apple pie with golden cheese—
Chocolate cake with chocolate icing,
Creamy custard, full of cherries,

And green cup cakes with his name spelled VERY LARGE in candy berries.

Just as he had finished eating, Cowboy Bill heard lots of noise; horns and drums and feet parading, and a band of big cowboys, clippy-clopping on their horses, came a-gallop up the street.

"Rodeo!" they called.

"It's starting at the fair grounds! Half-past one!"

Cowboy Bill rode out there with them.
He was ready for some fun.
First he won the pony races.
Then he won the shooting thing.

Then he won the prize for throwing wild bulls in the throwing ring.

Then he won the prize for roping,
And the wild horse riding prize,
And the prize for doing rope tricks.
All the cowboys blinked their eyes.

THEN he won the prize for jumping from one horse back to another. (The prize was a set of painted dishes that he took home to his mother.)

She was very glad to see him, and she liked her painted prize.

But she said it was past bedtime. She could tell it by his eyes.

Cowboy Bill put on pajamas, brushed his teeth, climbed into bed, with his blanket tucked around him and his pillow at his head.

And his head all full of outlaws, pie and cake and Indian bows, running steers and cheering cowboys, and new boots that pinched his toes.

And a gallop on the prairie.

And a gallop up the hill.

And how no one EVER argued with the daring Cowboy Bill.

1

By JANE WERNER

Illustrated by

AURELIUS BATTAGLIA

2

"It is high time you had a pet, Peter," said Peter's Daddy one day. "What kind would you like?"

"Let me see," said Peter. "I would like to try some out before I decide."

3

And away went Peter, to look for some pets. He started with an elephant. It was fun to ride down jungle paths on his great, gray head.

4

But back home there would be no place for an elephant to sleep.

5

Next he tried a camel, which is not so large. Peter rode on its back, between its high humps.

6

7

Peter tried to make friends with a lion, with a shaggy mane and a magnificent roar. And with a tawny, striped tiger. He thought he would like to be a famous lion and tiger trainer, and wear black boots and wave a chair. He would teach the animals to jump through hoops and things.

8

But the lion and tiger had a fierce and hungry look, for pets.

9

Peter met a striped zebra, running by on swift little hoofs.

"I would rather have a pony I could ride," Peter said. "And even a pony is not just what I want."

10

He tried a giraffe. It was gentle, and so out of reach. And the giraffe could not talk to him, at all.

11

Next he met a polar bear. "How would you like to be a pet?" asked Peter. "I would teach you to be a dancing bear. And people would clap when you danced."

12

But the bear was not interested. So Peter traveled on.

13

Out in the sea he met a seal.

14

"I could train you," said Peter. "You could balance a ball on the tip of your nose, and then I'd throw you a fish to eat."

But the seal Peter picked did not seem to want to learn.

15

He met a little spotted fawn that was sweet and shy. But it did not want to leave home to be a pet.

16

So Peter wandered on. He tried out a lamb, a frisky white lamb that would kick up its heels and play.

17

He tried making a pet of a long-legged calf. He fed it milk from a pail. And it followed him down the lane and mooed when it was hungry.

18

19

So Peter tried barnyard pets, chickens and turkeys and gray guinea hens.

20

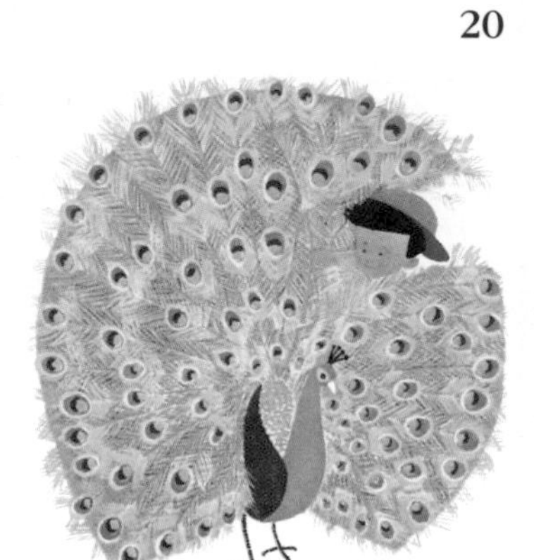

"But even a peacock," said Peter, "would not be much of a pet for me."

21

Down at the pond he found swans that floated, and ducklings that dove, and bullfrogs that swelled up their throats and croaked.

22

There were geese there, too, and turtles that snapped and lay on a log in the sun for a nap.

23

24

They were all very nice. But they were not the pets for Peter.

"I do not want a rhinoceros, either, or a hippopotamus, or even a kangaroo with a pouch full of bouncing babies," he said.

25

"I don't even want a cute little kitten that washes its face politely with its paws.

"And that's about all the kinds of pets I know—all but one," said Peter. "So I guess that one must be the best pet of them all for me!

26

"Yes, sir, Daddy," said Peter. "I know now what I want. I want a good old, little old—puppy dog!"

27

And that is exactly what Peter got!

Once there was a tawny, scrawny, hungry lion who never could get enough to eat.

He chased monkeys on Monday—kangaroos on Tuesday—zebras on Wednesday—bears on Thursday—camels on Friday—and on Saturday, elephants!

And since he caught everything he ran after, that lion should have been as fat as butter. But he wasn't at all. The more he ate, the scrawnier and hungrier he grew.

The other animals didn't feel one bit safe. They stood at a distance and tried to talk things over with the tawny, scrawny lion.

"It's all your fault for running away," he grumbled. "If I didn't have to run, run, run for every single bite I get, I'd be fat as butter and sleek as satin. Then I wouldn't have to eat so much, and you'd last longer!"

Just then, a fat little rabbit came hopping through the forest, picking berries. All the big animals looked at him and grinned slyly.

"Rabbit," they said. "Oh, you lucky rabbit! We appoint you to talk things over with the lion."

That made the little rabbit feel very proud.

"What shall I talk about?" he asked eagerly.

"Any old thing," said the big animals. "The important thing is to go right up close."

So the fat little rabbit hopped right up to the big hungry lion and counted his ribs.

"You look much too scrawny to talk things over," he said. "So how about supper at my house first?"

"What's for supper?" asked the lion.

The little rabbit said, "Carrot stew." That sounded awful to the lion. But the little rabbit said, "Yes sir, my five fat sisters and my four fat brothers are making a delicious big carrot stew right now!"

"What are we waiting for?" cried the lion. And he went hopping away with the little rabbit, thinking of ten fat rabbits, and looking just as jolly as you please.

"Well," grinned all the big animals. "That should take care of Tawny-Scrawny for today."

Before very long, the lion began to wonder if they would ever get to the rabbit's house.

First, the fat little rabbit kept stopping to pick berries and mushrooms and all sorts of good-smelling herbs. And when his basket was full, what did he do but flop down on the river bank!

"Wait a bit," he said. "I want to catch a few fish for the stew."

That was almost too much for the hungry lion.

For a moment, he thought he would have to eat that one little rabbit then and there. But he kept saying, "five fat sisters and four fat brothers" over and over to himself. And at last the two were on their way again.

"Here we are!" said the rabbit, hopping around a turn with the lion close behind him. Sure enough, there was the rabbit's house, with a big pot of carrot stew bubbling over an open fire.

And sure enough, there were nine more fat, merry little rabbits hopping around it!

When they saw the fish, they popped them into the stew, along with the mushrooms and herbs. The stew began to smell very good indeed.

And when they saw the tawny, scrawny lion, they gave him a big bowl of hot stew. And then they hopped about so busily, that really, it would have been quite a job for that tired, hungry lion to catch even one of them!

So he gobbled his stew, but the rabbits filled his bowl again. When he had eaten all he could hold, they heaped his bowl with berries.

And when the berries were gone—the tawny, scrawny lion wasn't scrawny any more! He felt so good and fat and comfortable that he couldn't even move.

"Here's a fine thing!" he said to himself. "All these fat little rabbits, and I haven't room inside for even one!"

He looked at all those fine, fat little rabbits and wished he'd get hungry again.

"Mind if I stay a while?" he asked.

"We wouldn't even hear of your going!" said the rabbits. Then they plumped themselves down in the lion's lap and began to sing songs.

And somehow, even when it was time to say goodnight, that lion wasn't one bit hungry!

Home he went, through the soft moonlight, singing softly to himself. He curled up in his bed, patted his sleek, fat tummy, and smiled.

When he woke up in the morning, it was Monday.

"Time to chase monkeys!" said the lion.

But he wasn't one bit hungry for monkeys! What he wanted was some more of that tasty carrot stew. So off he went to visit the rabbits.

On Tuesday he didn't want kangaroos, and on Wednesday he didn't want zebras. He wasn't hungry for bears on Thursday, or camels on Friday, or elephants on Saturday.

All the big animals were so surprised and happy!

They dressed in their best and went to see the fat little rabbit.

"Rabbit," they said. "Oh, you wonderful rabbit! What in the world did you talk to the tawny, scrawny, hungry, terrible lion about?"

That fat little rabbit jumped up in the air and said, "Oh, my goodness! We had such a good time with that nice, jolly lion that I guess we forgot to talk about anything at all!"

And before the big animals could say one word, the tawny lion came skipping up the path. He had a basket of berries for the fat rabbit sisters, and a string of fish for the fat rabbit brothers, and a big bunch of daisies for the fat rabbit himself.

"I came for supper," he said, shaking paws all around.

Then he sat down in the soft grass, looking fat as butter, sleek as satin, and jolly as all get out, all ready for another good big supper of carrot stew.

WHEELS

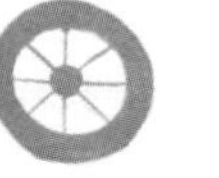

By KATHRYN JACKSON

Illustrated by
LEONARD WEISGARD

A wheelbarrow runs on just one wheel.
A bicycle goes on two.
A tricycle needs all three of its wheels.
Take one off, and down goes you!

A car has two big wheels in front
and two big wheels in back,
and a spare in case one goes flat,
and a steering wheel for steering with,
and a horn that goes beep! like that.

There are four wheels each on
roller skates.
"Come on, let's have a race!"
And the clock has dozens of busy wheels
in back of its quiet face.

A motorcycle has two swift wheels,
and sometimes a seat on the side.
"Hop in, hold tight and hold your hat—
I'll take you for a ride!"

Some wheels go up.
Some wheels go down.
The clothesline goes around.
"I'll make it roll—
you hang the clothes—
don't let them touch the ground!"

A tractor has a steering wheel
and four big wheels that run.
The lawnmower wheels turn its
cutting blades
and all sparkly in the sun
is the water on the big boat wheels
as they go splashing round.

A water wheel runs the old stone mill
where pancake flour is ground.
And next comes a wheel
that's a sideways wheel.
Of course, it's a merry-go-round!

The grocery cart has four low wheels.
A ride in it is lots of fun!
And the trolley car has one
high-up wheel.
That's the one that makes it run.

A truck has double wheels in back—
a big bus has them, too.
But the fastest wheels are the eight
red wheels on the hook and ladder
—whoooo!

The ferris wheel is the biggest wheel
that ever was anywhere.
It takes you up, and up, and up
for a ride high in the air!

And when you're in bed, a silvery wheel
rolls slowly across the sky, while all sorts
of wheels go by in the dark.
You can hear them if you try.

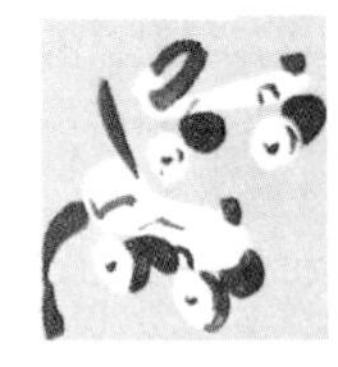

LITTLE BOY WITH A BIG HORN

By JACK BECHDOLT

Illustrated by AURELIUS BATTAGLIA

Ollie was learning to play the bass horn. Ollie was a small boy. And the horn was a big horn.

He knew only one tune. It was called "Asleep in the Deep." It told about a shipwreck and brave sailors.

Maybe you know that tune.

The music goes way down deep, like this:

"MANY BRAVE HEARTS
ARE ASLEEP IN THE DEEP SO BEWARE
BEEEE
E
E
E
WARE!"

Ollie loved that song, but . . .

Ollie's mother said, "Please, NOT in the house, Ollie. I can't think straight about my housework."

"Yes, Mother," said Ollie and took his horn into the back yard.

"Beeeeee-ware . . . BEEEE-WARE!" boomed the big horn.

"Owroooo!" howled all the town dogs.

"Oh bother!" said all the neighbors.

"MANY
BRAVE HEARTS
ARE ASLEEP IN
THE DEEP SO
BEWARE
BEEEEE
E
E
E
WARE!"

The Grocer dropped a crate of eggs.

The Preacher couldn't write his sermon.

The Farmer's horses ran away.

Everybody agreed that the town must do something to stop Ollie from playing that horn.

All together they called on Ollie's mother.

"We love music," they said, "but too much is TOO MUCH!"

"But the boy must practice," said Ollie's mother.

"Perhaps, but not here," said the neighbors.

"We must think of a better place," said Ollie's mother.

"Yes, yes, a better place," they all agreed. "But where?" Everyone thought hard.

"I have it," Ollie cried.

Everybody stopped thinking and looked at him.

"I'll go way off in the fields. Nobody can hear me there."

"Splendid!" said everybody.

"Wonderful idea!" they agreed.

"Ollie is a good boy," said his proud mother.

Ollie set out for the distant pastures.

The sun was hot.

He grew tired. But he kept on.

Far from home, he stopped at last.

He spread out his music and took up his horn.

First he played, "Unk . . . unk . . . UNK."

Then he played "Asleep in the Deep."

Surely nobody would mind now, for there was nobody to mind!

But somebody did mind!

Over the hill the Farmer's cows were grazing.

"Beeeeee-WARE!" boomed the big horn.

The cattle raised their heads.

They had never heard the like of it.

They began to gather from near and far. They began to move toward the strange noise.

"Moo!" said one.

"Arooo!" bawled another.

The busy Farmer heard them.

"Drat," he said. "The old muley has fallen into the ditch again."

Pitchfork in hand, he came running to rescue his cows.

When he saw Ollie, the Farmer was angry.

"You can't play that horn here," he said. "It's enough to sour their milk."

"Oh, dear," sighed Ollie.

He picked up his horn and turned homeward.

The sun shone hot on his back.

He was thirsty. And tired.

"Seems as if there is no place in the world where I can learn to play my horn," he sighed.

And then he had another bright idea. Far off he saw the ocean.

"I'll go down to the ocean," said Ollie. "There's nobody there but fish and seagulls, and they won't mind my music."

So he went and got his rowboat and began to row far out from the shore.

Some dangerous rocks marked the entrance to the harbor.

The rocks were guarded by a bell buoy that tolled a warning to incoming vessels.

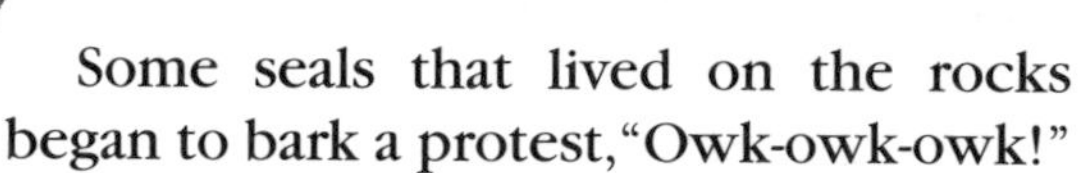

But when Ollie reached the rocks the bell buoy was not there. It had drifted away.

There was nothing to warn the vessels.

And now a thick fog was spreading over the ocean.

It shut out sight of everything, even the rocks near by.

Every day at this time a steamship brought passengers and freight to the town where Ollie lived.

The ship must be somewhere near even now, lost in the fog.

There was no warning bell to tell its captain when he was near the rocks.

The ship might strike on the reef.

"I'll stay here and play on my horn," Ollie decided. "That will be a warning."

So Ollie stayed. And he played.

He played "Asleep in the Deep," because that was the only tune he knew.

A big gray gull circled over his head. Then another. And another.

"Awk-awk-awk-awk," they shouted angrily.

Some seals that lived on the rocks began to bark a protest, "Owk-owk-owk!"

"I am very sorry if you don't like my music," said Ollie politely, "but I'm NOT going away."

He kept right on playing to warn the lost ship of her danger.

The ship was drawing closer.

The captain peered through the fog.

He and his crew could see nothing.

They listened for the bell buoy's warning.

They could hear nothing but the sea.

But what was that noise?

"Bee-WARE!" boomed Ollie's big horn.

The men on the ship were amazed.

"Stop the ship," cried the Captain. "Lower a boat and find out what's making music out here on the ocean."

And that was how they found Ollie and escaped being wrecked upon the rocks.

"We owe our lives to this brave boy," said the steamship Captain.

All the passengers cheered.

When the ship reached her dock all the town heard of Ollie's brave deed.

"He must be rewarded," they said.

And a big public meeting was held at the Town Hall.

The Mayor gave Ollie a handsome medal marked

"FOR BRAVERY"

and said the town would send Ollie to music school.

Ollie thanked the Mayor.

"I will be able to play my horn as much as I like," he said. "And the school is so far from our town that nobody will be disturbed any more."

Everybody cheered and said that Ollie was as wise as he was brave.

A boy had a secret. It was a surprise.
He wanted to tell his grandmother.
So he sent his secret through the mail.
The story of that letter
Is the reason for this tale

By MARGARET WISE BROWN
and EDITH THACHER HURD
Illustrated by TIBOR GERGELY

Of the seven little postmen who carried
The mail.
Because there was a secret in the letter.
The boy sealed it with red sealing wax.
If anyone broke the seal
The secret would be out.
He slipped the letter into the mail box.
The first little postman
Took it from the box,
Put it in his bag,
And walked
Seventeen blocks
To a big Post Office
All built of rocks.
The letter with the
Secret
Was dumped on a
Table
With big and small letters
That all needed the label
Of the big Post Office.
Stamp stamp, clickety click,
The machinery ran with a quick sharp
Tick.

The letter with the secret is stamped
At last
And the round black circle tells that it
Passed
Through the
Canceling machine
Whizz whizz fast!
Big letters
Small letters
Thin and tall—

The second little postman
Sorts them all.
The letters are sorted
From East to West
From North to South.

"And this letter
Had best go West,"
Said the second
Little postman,
Scratching his chest.
Into the pouch
Lock it tight
The secret letter
Must travel all night.
The third little postman in the
Big mail car
Comes to a crossroad where
Waiting are
A green, a yellow, and a purple car.
They all stop there.
There is nothing to say.
The mail truck has the right of way!
"The mail must go through!"
Up and away through sleet and hail
This airplane carries the fastest mail.
The pilot flies through whirling snow
As far and as fast as the plane can go.
And he drops the mail for the evening
Train.
Now hang the pouch on the big hook
Crane!
The engine speeds up the shining rails
And the fourth little postman
Grabs the mail with a giant hook.

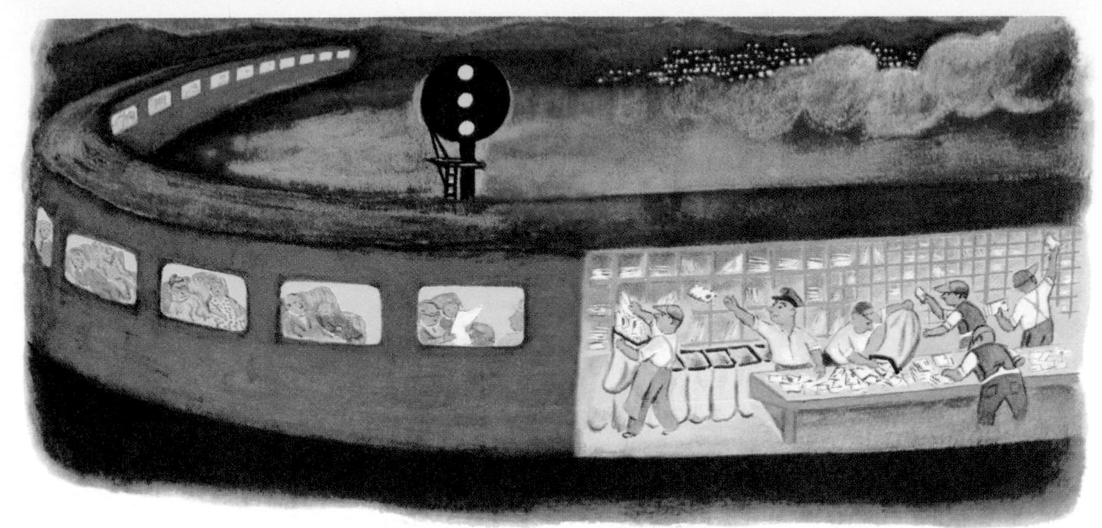

The train roars on
With a puff and a snort
And the fourth little postman
Begins to sort.
The train carries the letters
Through gloom of night
In a mail car filled with electric light
To a country postman
By a country road
Where the fifth little postman
Is waiting for his load.
The mail clerk
Heaves the mail pouch
With all his might
To the fifth little postman
Who grabs it tight.
Then off he goes
Along the lane
And over the hill
Until
He comes to a little town
That is very small—
So very small
The Post Office there
Is hardly one at all.
The sixth little postman
In great big boots
Sorts the letters
For their various routes—
Some down the river,
Some over the hill.
But the secret letter
Goes farther still.

The seventh little postman on R.F.D.
Carries letters and papers, chickens and
Fruit
To the people who live along his route.
He stops to deliver some sugar
To Mr. Jones who keeps a store
And always seems to need something
More.
For Mrs. O'Finnigan with all her ills
He brings a bottle of bright pink pills,
And an airmail letter that cost seven
Cents
He hands to a farmer over the fence.
There were parts for a tractor
And a wig for an actor
And a funny post card for a little boy

Playing in his own backyard.

There was something for Sally

And something for Sam

And something for Mrs. Potter
Who was busy making jam.
There were dozens of chickens for Mrs.
Pickens
And a dress for a party for Mrs. McCarty.
There was a special delivery—crisp orange
and blue.
What was the hurry, nobody knew.

At the last house along the way sat the grandmother of the boy who had sent the letter with the secret in it. She had been wishing all day he would come to visit. For she lived all alone in a tiny house and was sometimes lonely.

The Postman blew his whistle and gave her the letter with the red sealing wax on it—the secret letter!

"Sakes alive! What is it about?"

Sakes Alive! The secret is out! What does it say?

SEVEN LITTLE POSTMEN

Seven Little Postmen carried the mail
Through Rain and Snow and Wind and Hail
Through Snow and Rain and Gloom of Night
Seven Little Postmen
Out of sight.
Over Land and Sea
Through Air and Light
Through Snow and Rain
And Gloom of Night—
Put a stamp on your letter
And seal it tight.

MISTER DOG

The Dog Who Belonged to Himself

By MARGARET WISE BROWN

Illustrated by GARTH WILLIAMS

Once upon a time there was a funny dog named Crispin's Crispian. He was named Crispin's Crispian because—
he belonged to himself.

In the mornings he woke himself up and he went to the icebox and gave himself some bread and milk. He was a funny old dog. He liked strawberries.

Then he took himself for a walk. And he went wherever he wanted to go.

But one morning he didn't know where he wanted to go.

"Just walk and sooner or later you'll get somewhere," he said to himself.

Soon he came to a country where there were lots of dogs. They barked at him and he barked back. Then they all played together.

But he still wanted to go somewhere so he walked on until he came to a country where there were lots of cats and rabbits.

The cats and rabbits jumped in the air and ran. So Crispian jumped in the air and ran after them.

He didn't catch them because he ran bang into a little boy.

"Who are you and who do you belong to?" asked the little boy.

"I am Crispin's Crispian and I belong to myself," said Crispian. "Who and what are you?"

"I am a boy," said the boy, "and I belong to myself."

"I am so glad," said Crispin's Crispian. "Come and live with me."

So the boy walked on with Crispian and threw him sticks to chase, all through the shining, sun-drenched morning.

"I'm hungry," said Crispin's Crispian.

"I'm hungry, too," said the boy's little boy.

So they went to a butcher shop—"to get this poor dog a bone," Crispian said.

Now since Crispin's Crispian belonged to himself, he gave himself the bone and trotted home with it.

And the boy bought a big lamb chop

and a bright green vegetable and trotted home with Crispin's Crispian.

Crispin's Crispian lived in a two-story doghouse in a garden.

And in his two-story doghouse he had a little fur living room with a warm fire that crackled all winter and went out in the summer.

His house was always warm. His house had a chimney for the smoke to go out.

And there was plenty of room in his house for the boy to live there with him.

Crispian went upstairs, and the boy went with him.

And upstairs he had a little bedroom with a bed in it and a place for his leash and a pillow under which he hid his bones.

And he had windows to look out of and a garden to run around in any time he felt like running around in it. The garden was blooming with dogwood and dogtooth violets.

And he had a little kitchen upstairs in his two-story doghouse where he fixed himself a good dinner three times a day because he liked to eat. He liked steaks and chops and roast beef and chopped meat and raw eggs.

This evening he made a bone soup with lots of meat in it. He gave some to the boy and the boy liked it. The boy didn't give Crispian his chop bone but he put some of his bright green vegetables in the soup.

And what did Crispian do with his dinner?

Did he put it in his stomach?

Yes, indeed.

He chewed it up and swallowed it into his little fat stomach.

And what did the little boy do with his dinner?

Did he put it into his stomach?

Yes, indeed.

He chewed it up and swallowed it into his little fat stomach.

Crispin's Crispian was a *conservative*. He liked everything at the right time—

dinner at dinnertime,
lunch at lunchtime,
breakfast in time for breakfast,
and sunrise at sunrise,
and sunset at sunset.
And at bedtime—

At bedtime he liked everything in its own place—

the cup in the saucer,
the chair under the table,
the stars in the heavens,
the moon in the sky,
and himself in his own little bed.

And then what did he do?

Then he curled in a warm little heap and went to sleep. And he dreamed his own dreams.

That was what the dog who belonged to himself did.

And what did the boy who belonged to himself do? The boy who belonged to himself curled in a warm little heap and went to sleep. And he dreamed his own dreams.

That was what the boy who belonged to himself did.

Wiggles

By LOUISE WOODCOCK

Illustrated by ELOISE WILKIN

One day Donnie went with his mother to see Mrs. Jones. Mrs. Jones lived on a farm. Donnie had never been there before.

Mrs. Jones said, "I'm so glad to see you, Donnie; go hunt around outdoors. You will find Wiggles to play with you."

Donnie didn't know who Wiggles was. A dog? A cat? A lamb? Or a mouse?

He could have asked Mrs. Jones but he didn't like to.

So he went out to look around.

The first thing he saw was a rabbit hutch. A big white rabbit was nibbling lettuce.

Could this rabbit be Wiggles? wondered Donnie.

Just then a big girl came from the barn. She was carrying eggs in a basket.

"Has this rabbit a name?" asked Donnie.

"We just call him Pinky," said the girl. "Because of his big pink ears."

She went on into the house.

A squirrel whisked up a tree and sat on a branch over Donnie's head. He chattered and wiggled and twitched his tail.

Could he be Wiggles? wondered Donnie.

Just then a big boy came round the barn.

"Has that squirrel a name?" asked Donnie.

"Not that I know of," said the boy. "Most squirrels don't. Not wild ones anyway."

He went along to the pump.

Donnie walked past the barn. There in a pen were five little piglets with their mother. The piglets poked and nosed and wiggled their little curly tails.

Could all these little pigs be Wiggles? wondered Donnie.

There was an old man sitting near by on a chopping block.

"Have these little pigs got names?" asked Donnie.

"Not yet, son," the old man said and went on sitting.

Donnie walked on along a lane and wondered and wondered.

Could Wiggles be these butterflies hovering over the clover?

Could Wiggles be these little chickens pecking, pecking?

Could this old mother hen be Wiggles?

Or the great rooster strutting around with his handsome tail?

How could you play with butterflies, or little chicks that ran so fast, or mother hens who squawked and fluttered away, or that big rooster looking proud and fierce?

Donnie walked on till he saw some cows in a field. A baby calf with wobbly legs was standing by its mother. There was a man there too, stroking the little calf's neck.

Could that calf be Wiggles? wondered Donnie.

"Has that little calf got a name?" he called to the man.

"My wife just calls him Pet," the man shouted back.

"Why don't you go find Wiggles? Down in the orchard."

Donnie wanted to ask him, "Who is Wiggles?"

He was afraid it might sound silly, so he walked toward the orchard.

There was a curly-haired dog just coming out of the orchard. He was sniffing the ground sniff-sniff-sniff-sniff. Could this be Wiggles? wondered Donnie. All the dogs he knew had names. This one's might be Wiggles.

Then a little old woman hobbled out of the orchard. She was carrying apples in her apron.

Donnie asked her, "What is that dog's name, please?"

"Have an apple?" asked the little old woman, holding out her apron.

"Thank you," Donnie said and took one.

"His name's Jip," the old woman said. "Why don't you go find Wiggles? Last tree down this row. Come, Jip." She hobbled away. Jip trotted after her.

Donnie wondered what she could mean about the tree. Could Wiggles be a bird? How could you play with a bird?

He walked along the row of trees until he came to the last one. There was a ladder leaning against it.

"Hi!" said a voice up among the branches. "Want to come up in my treehouse?"

Donnie looked up and saw a boy looking down through the leaves.

"My name's Donnie. What's yours?" asked Donnie. He put one foot on the ladder.

"Wiggles," the boy replied. "Did you ever have a treehouse?"

"No," said Donnie. He climbed another step. "But why do they call you Wiggles?" he asked.

"Oh, just because I can wiggle my ears. Come up and I'll show you," Wiggles said.

So Donnie climbed up where he could see and Wiggles showed him.

DADDIES

By JANET FRANK

Illustrated by

TIBOR GERGELY

What do Daddies do all day?
Daddies work while children play.
They work at desks.
They work in stores,
in factories
and out-of-doors.

Daddies fix the clothes we wear.
Barber Daddies cut our hair.
Some Daddies help us keep well-fed.
They make buns and cakes and bread.

Some build planes.
Some make them fly.
Some catch fish for us to fry.

Dads make clocks
and Dads make chairs.
Farmer Dads grow corn and pears.

Dads are sailors dressed in blue.
And Daddies are policemen, too.
Some Daddies mend our broken toys.
And some teach little girls and boys.

Dads dig coal
and Dads drive cars.
Dads put food in cans and jars.

Doctor Daddies keep folks well.
Daddies paint
and Daddies sell.
Daddies sit at desks and write
the books we read in bed each night.

Dads make steel
and Daddies sing.
Dads do almost everything.
But when they've worked the whole
day through
what do they like best to do?
By taxi, train, by car and bus,
Daddy rushes home—to us!

Born at sea in the teeth of a gale, the sailor was a dog. Scuppers was his name.

After that he lived on a farm. But Scuppers, born at sea, was a sailor. And when he grew up he wanted to go to sea.

So he went to look for something to go in.

He found a big airplane. "All aboard!" they called. It was going up in the sky. But Scuppers did not want to go up in the sky.

He found a little submarine. "All aboard!" they called. It was going down under the sea. But Scuppers did not want to go under the sea.

He found a little car.

"All aboard!" they called. It was going over the land. But Scuppers did not want to go over the land.

He found a subway train.

"All aboard!" they called. It was going under the earth. But Scuppers did not want to go under the earth.

Scuppers was a sailor. He wanted to go to sea.

So Scuppers went over the hills and far away until he came to the sea.

Over the hills and far away was the ocean. And on the ocean was a ship. The ship was about to go over the sea. It blew all its whistles.

"All aboard!" they called.

"All ashore that are going ashore!"

"All aboard!"

So Scuppers went to sea.

The ship began to move slowly along. The wind blew it.

In his ship Scuppers had a little room. In his room Scuppers had a hook for his hat and a hook for his rope and a hook for his handkerchief and a hook for his pants and a hook for his spyglass and a place for his shoes and a bunk for a bed to put himself in.

At night Scuppers threw the anchor into the sea and he went down to his little room.

He put his hat on the hook for his hat, and his rope on the hook for his rope, and his pants on the hook for his pants, and his spyglass on the hook for his spyglass, and he put his shoes under the bed, and got into his bed, which was a bunk, and went to sleep.

Next morning he was shipwrecked.

Too big a storm blew out of the sky. The anchor dragged and the ship crashed onto the rocks. There was a big hole in it.

Scuppers himself was washed overboard and hurled by huge waves onto the shore.

He was washed up onto the beach. It was foggy and rainy. There were no houses and Scuppers needed a house.

But on the beach was lots and lots of driftwood, and he found an old rusty box stuck in the sand.

Maybe it was a treasure!

It was a treasure—to Scuppers.

It was an old-fashioned tool box with hammers and nails and an ax and a saw.

Everything he needed to build himself a house. So Scuppers started to build a house, all by himself, out of driftwood.

He built a door and a window and a roof and a porch and a floor, all out of driftwood.

And he found some red bricks and built a big red chimney. And then he lit a fire and the smoke went up the chimney.

After building his house he was hungry. So he went fishing. He went fishing in a big river. The first fish he caught never came up. The second fish he caught got away. The third fish he caught was too little, but the next fish he caught was—just right.

Then he cooked the fish he caught in

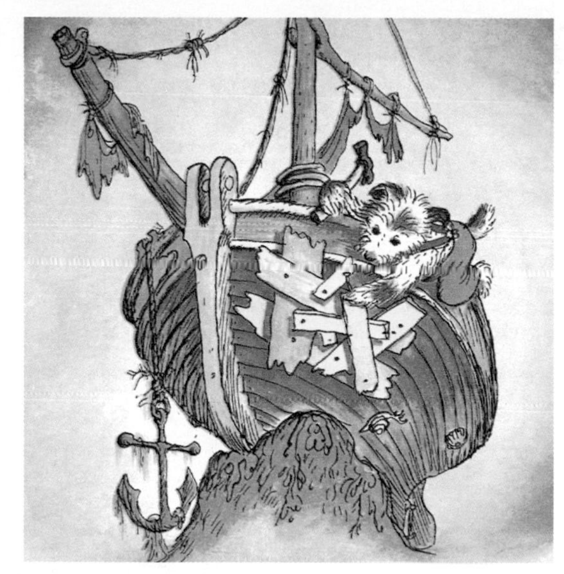

the house he built, and smoke went up the chimney.

Then the stars came out and he was sleepy. So he built a bed of pine branches.

And he jumped into his deep green bed and went to sleep. As he slept he dreamed—

If he could build a house
he could mend the hole in the ship.

So the next day at low tide he took his tool box and waded out and hammered planks across the hole in his ship.

At last the ship was fixed.

So he sailed away.

Until he came to a seaport in a foreign land.

By now his clothes were all worn and ripped and torn and blown to pieces. His coat was torn, his hat was blown away, and his shoes were all worn out. And his handkerchief was ripped. Only his pants were still good.

So he went ashore to buy some clothes at the Army and Navy Store. And some fresh oranges. He bought a coat. He found a red one too small. He found a blue one just right. It had brass buttons on it.

Then he went to buy a hat. He found a purple one too silly. He found a white one just right.

He needed new shoes. He found some yellow ones too small. He found some red ones too fancy. Then he found some white ones just right.

Here he is with his new hat on, and with his new shoes on, and with his new coat on, with his shiny brass buttons. (He has a can of polish and a cloth to keep them shiny.)

And he has a new clean handkerchief, and a new rope, and a bushel of oranges.

And now Scuppers wants to go back to his ship. So he goes there.

And at night when the stars came out, he took one last look through his spyglass. And went down below to his little room, and he hung his new hat on the hook for the hat, and he hung his spyglass on the hook for his spyglass, and he hung his new coat on the hook for his coat, and his new handkerchief on the hook for his handkerchief, and his pants on the hook for his pants, and his new rope on the hook for his rope, and his new shoes he put under his bunk, and himself he put in his bunk.

And here he is where he wants to be—
A sailor sailing the deep green Sea.

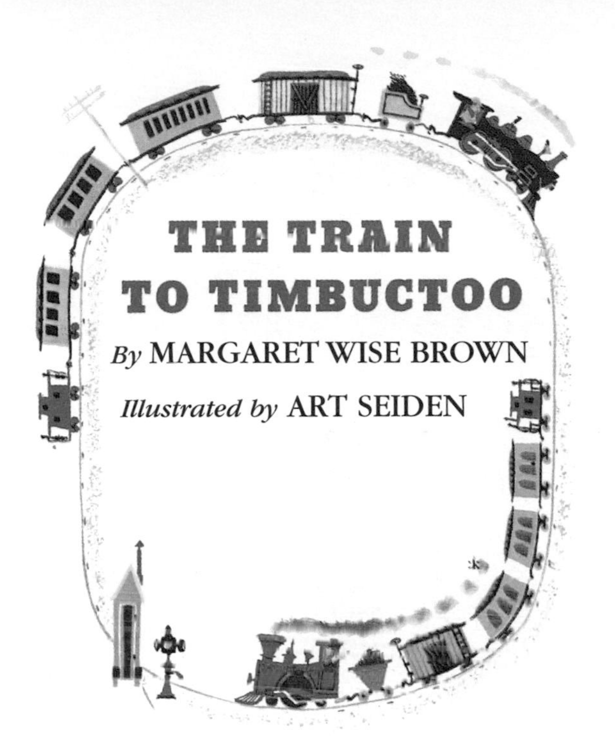

THE TRAIN TO TIMBUCTOO

By MARGARET WISE BROWN

Illustrated by ART SEIDEN

Clackety clack—clackety clack
There was a big train
and clickety click clickety click—clickety click
There was a very little train.
They were on their way
home to Timbuctoo.
And they had just left
the town of Kalamazoo.
Slam Bang grease the engine
throw out the throttle
and give it the gun.
There was a big engineer
who drove the big engine.
And Slam Bang grease the engine
throw out the throttle
and give it the gun.
There was a little engineer
who drove the little engine.
When the big engine
went through a tunnel
The big engineer blew his big whistle
whooooooooooooooooooooooooo
When the little engine
went through a tunnel
The little engineer blew his whistle
wheeeeeeeeeeeeeeeeeeeeeeeeeeeeeeeeeeeee
And clackety clack—clickety click
Throw out the throttle
and give it the gun
whoooooooooooooooooooooooooo
wheeeeeeeeeeeeeeeeeeeeeeeeeeeeeeeeeeeeeeee
Out from the big tunnel
came the big engine
With the big engineer
And the big coal car
And the big baggage car
And the big passenger car
And the big dining car
And the big sleeping car
And a little caboose

And then out from the little tunnel
came the little engine
With the little engineer
And the little coal car
And the little baggage car
And the little passenger car
And the little dining car
And the little sleeping car
And a little caboose
Clickety click—clickety click
clackety clack—clackety clack
whoooooooooooooooooooooooooo
wheeeeeeeeeeeeeeeeeeeeeeeeeeeeeeeeeeeeeee
That great big train and that little tiny
train went roaring by.
Then clackety clack—clackety clack
The big train came to a big bridge
over a big river
And over the big bridge
went the big engine
With the big engineer
And the big coal car
And the big baggage car
And the big passenger car
And the big dining car
And the big sleeping car
And a little caboose

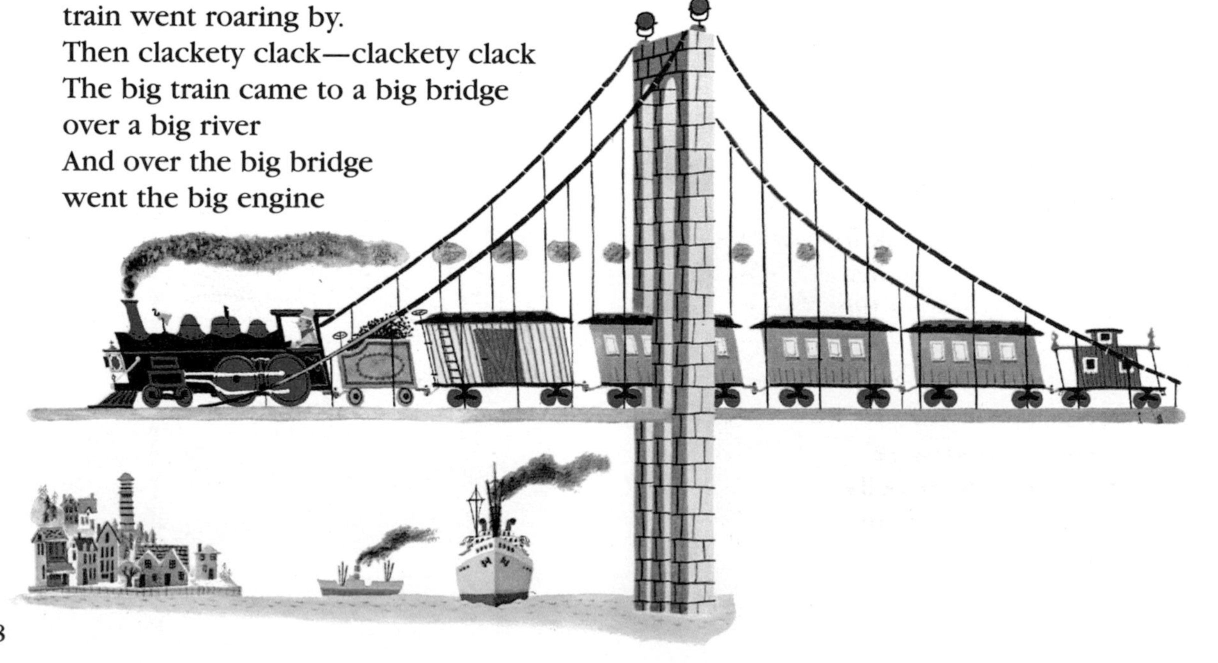

Then
Clickety click—clickety click
The little train came to a little bridge
Over a river, over a little river,
And clickety click—clickety click
Over the little bridge
went the little engine
With the little engineer
And the little coal car
And the little baggage car
And the little passenger car
And the little dining car
And the little sleeping car
And a little caboose
And clickety click—clickety click
clackety clack—clackety clack—
pocketa—pocketa—pocketa—
pocketa
picketa—picketa—picketa—picketa
The trains rolled on towards
Timbuctoo
Far down the track from Kalamazoo
Until far away against the sky
There was a great big railroad station
And far away against the sky
There was a little railroad station.
whooooooooooo
wheeeeeeeeeeeeeeeee
As ringing their bells
dong—dong—dong
ding—ding—ding

That great big train
with a puff—puff—puff
And that tiny little train
with a piff—piff—piff
Came home to Timbuctoo.
And if you switch
the names of the towns
in the front of the book
You can get back to
Kalamazoo.

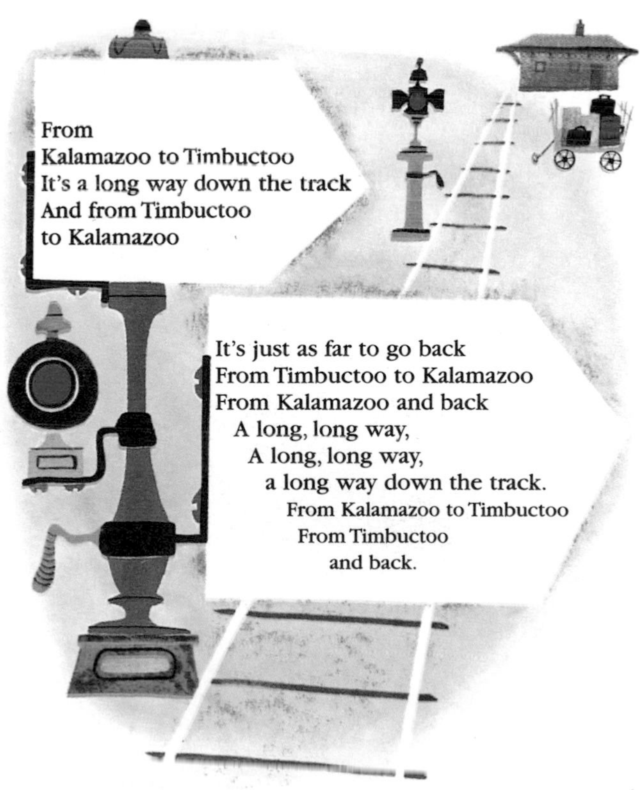

THE FUZZY DUCKLING

By JANE WERNER

Illustrated by

ALICE *and* MARTIN PROVENSEN

Early one bright morning a small fuzzy duckling went for a walk.
He walked through the sunshine.
He walked through the shade.
In the long striped shadows that the cattails made he met two frisky colts.
"Hello," said the duckling.
"Will you come for a walk with me?"
But the two frisky colts would not.
So on went the little duckling,
on over the hill.
There he found three spotted calves,
all resting in the shade.
"Hello," said the duckling.
"Will you come for a walk with me?"
But the sleepy calves would not.
So on went the duckling.
He met four noisy turkeys and five white geese and six lively lambs with thick soft fleece.
But no one would come for a walk with the fuzzy duckling.
So on he went, all by his lone.
Poor little duckling.
He walked this way and that, but he could not find the right path.
He met seven playful puppies and eight hungry pigs.
"Won't you come for a walk with me?"
asked the fuzzy duckling.
"You had better walk straight home,"
said the pigs.
"Don't you know it's supper time?"
"Oh," said the duckling. "Thank you."
And he turned around to start for home.
But which way was home?
Just as he began to feel quite unhappy, he heard a sound in the rushes near by and out waddled nine fuzzy ducklings with their big mother duck.
"At last," said the mother duck.
"There is our lost baby duckling."
"Get in line," called the other ducklings.
"We're going home for supper."
So the lost little duckling joined the line, and away went the ten little ducklings, home for supper.
"This is the best way to go for a walk,"
said the happy little, fuzzy little duck.

THE MERRY SHIPWRECK

By GEORGES DUPLAIX

Illustrated by TIBOR GERGELY

Life was very peaceful on the barge.

Every morning Captain Barnacle would look at the East River and cock his weather eye. He knew whether it would rain before night.

When it did rain, the crew huddled around him while he spun a salty yarn about far-away places, shipwrecks, and oceans. Why, one would think the world was full of oceans!

"Hee-haw!" laughed the donkey, quite sure there was no such thing as a shipwreck. The kittens snuggled closer to their mother. But the ducklings could hardly wait to grow up and sail the seven seas!

On clear mornings, after Captain Barnacle had listened to all the Shipping News on the radio, he went off to market, and to chat with the crew's many friends ashore.

But one day, while Captain Barnacle was away, mother mouse crept into the galley. And while she ate a piece of cheese, her little mice were sharpening their teeth on the rope that held the barge fast to the pier.

Suddenly—before the parrot could say "Jack Robinson!"—the rope snapped, and the barge was heading down the river!

What a lark! All the animals hung over the side to wave good-by to Captain Barnacle who was just coming back with his basket.

The cow steered, the donkey poled, and the pig waved a towel at all the tugs they passed.

They reached the end of the river, and traveling was such fun that no one noticed when the sun slipped under a cloud.

The sky grew dark. Soon there was thunder and lightning and wind and rain. Big waves slapped against the barge, rolling it this way and that.

The crew bellowed and barked and bleated and meowed for dear life.

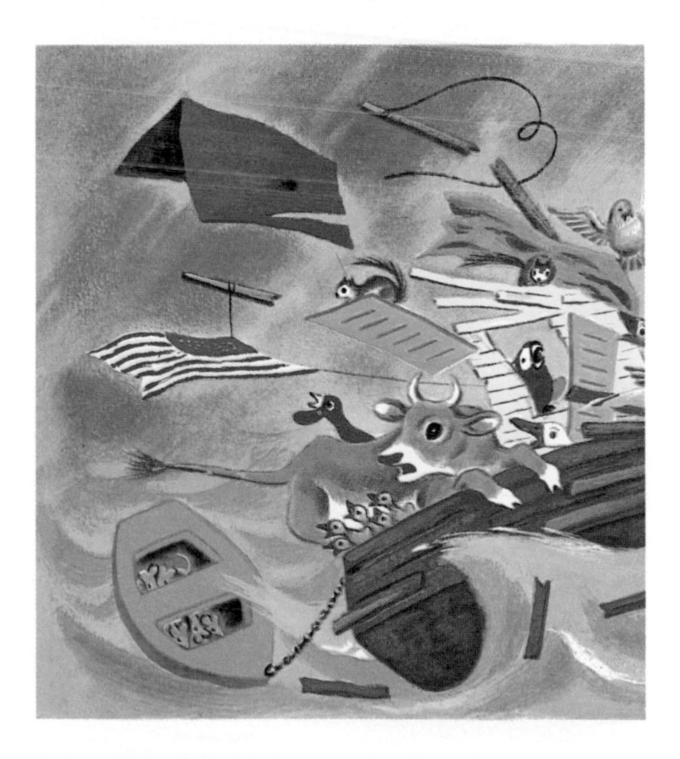

Finally, after tossing the helpless barge on a rock, the storm passed by. But there they were, shipwrecked and lost at sea, and very unhappy. Only the ducks didn't mind being soaking wet.

Many hours passed. At last they heard a boat whistle.

"Hurrah!" cried all the animals. "We're saved!"

Just then the sun came out again and they saw a red Fireboat, which was coming to their rescue.

"Come aboard!" cried the Fire Chief.

And whom did they find on the boat but Captain Barnacle! He had been looking for them everywhere.

Soon they were scampering all over the Fireboat. The donkey aimed the hose at the sky, the goat paraded the deck in fireman's hat and boots, and the hens roosted on top of the red funnel.

Then, "Bong, bong, bong!" the cabin boy called everybody to dinner. After dinner they went for a ride around the harbor, past ferryboats, tugs, tankers, yachts, battleships, rowboats, coal barges, liners, and freighters. But the Fireboat, looking like a red-and-gold Circus Boat, was far and away the finest of all.

At last everyone decided to have a look at the Statue of Liberty, and they sailed right up to it, landing on the little island underneath.

"Well, by cracky!" the keeper of the Statue of Liberty exclaimed. "Looks more like Noah's Ark than a Fireboat!"

On their way back they tied up alongside the battered barge. Poor Captain Barnacle looked very sad indeed.

"My poor barge!" he sobbed. "She was such a beautiful tub!"

"Never mind," said the Fire Chief. "Between your crew and mine we'll soon fix that!"

The firemen gave the animals lots of bright red paint, and a shiny brass bell to hang over the galley door. And they all went to work.

When everything was finished, Captain Barnacle was pleased as punch. And so were the animals.

Then they thanked the firemen and clanged their new bell for a last good-by.

The animals were so happy to go home that they sang and shouted all the way up the East River. They made so much noise that their friends on shore heard them, and hurried down to the dock.

The butcher was there, and the grocer, and the junkman with his horse.

The window cleaner, the mailman, the delivery boy, and the Good Humor man were there. So was Tony the fruit man—along with all the boys and girls and alley cats in the neighborhood.

"It's good to be home!" said Captain Barnacle, shaking hands around. "Let's have a party!"

"Yes, let's!" everybody shouted. "Let's have a party! Hip, hip, hooray!"

They decorated the barge with Chinese lanterns, and Captain Barnacle cooked the best supper ever cooked in his little galley.

Just as he was ringing the bell, the firemen arrived and joined the party.

Before long, everyone was dancing around the deck, and singing songs in the moonlight.

And that night, while Captain Barnacle and his crew were dreaming rosy dreams, the little mice were also quietly asleep. They would never, never again sharpen their teeth on the rope that held them so safely to shore!

By MARGARET WISE BROWN

Illustrated by GARTH WILLIAMS

I like cars
Red cars Green cars
Sport limousine cars
I like cars
A car in a garage
A car with a load
A car with a flat tire
A car on the road
I like cars.

I like trains
Express trains
Toy trains
Streamline trains
Freight trains
Old trains
Milk trains
Any kind of train
A train in the station
Trains crossing the plains
Trains in a snowstorm
Trains in the rain
I like trains.

I like stars
Yellow stars
Green stars
Red stars
Blue stars
I like stars
Far stars
Quiet stars
Bright stars
Light stars
I like stars
A star that is shooting across the dark sky
A star that is shining right straight in your eye
I like stars.

I like snow
Cold snow
Slow snow
White snow
Icy snow
I like snow

Snow falling softly
With everything still
White in the blue night,
White on the sill
White on the trees
On the far distant hill
With everything still
I like snow.

I like seeds
Mustard seeds Radish seeds
Corn seeds Flower seeds
Any kind of seed
Seeds that are sprouting green
From the ground
And seeds of the milkweed
Flying around
I like seeds.

I like bugs
Black bugs Green bugs
Bad bugs Mean bugs
Any kind of bug
A bug in a rug
A bug in the grass
A bug on the sidewalk
A bug in a glass
I like bugs
Round bugs Shiny bugs
Fat bugs Buggy bugs
Big bugs Lady bugs
I like bugs.

I like fish
Silver fish Gold fish
Black fish Old fish
Young fish Fishy fish
Any kind of fish

A fish in a pond
A fish in a stream
A fish in an ocean
A fish in a dream
I like fish.

I like boats
Any kind of boat
Tug boats Tow boats
Large boats Barge boats
Sail boats Whale boats
Thin boats Skin boats
Rubber boats River boats
Flat boats Cat boats
U-boats New boats
Tooting boats Hooting boats
South American fruit boats
Bum boats Gun boats
Slow boats Row boats
I like boats.

I like people
Glad people
Sad people
Slow people
Mad people
Big people
Little people
I like people.

I like whistles
Wild whistles Bird whistles
Far-off heard whistles
Boat whistles Train whistles
I like whistles
The postman's whistle
The policeman's whistle
The wind that blows away the thistle
Light as the little birds whistle and sing
And the little boy whistling in the spring
The wind that whistles through the trees
And blows the boats across the seas
I like whistles.

I like dogs
Big dogs Little dogs
Fat dogs Doggy dogs
Old dogs Puppy dogs
A dog that is barking over the hill
A dog that is dreaming very still
A dog that is running
Wherever he will
I like dogs.

THE KITTEN
who thought he was a
MOUSE

By MIRIAM NORTON

Illustrated by GARTH WILLIAMS

There were five Miggses: Mother and Father Miggs and Lester and two sisters.

They had, as field mice usually do, an outdoor nest for summer in an empty lot and an indoor nest for winter in a nearby house.

They were very surprised one summer day to find a strange bundle in their nest, a small gray and black bundle of fur and ears and legs, with eyes not yet open. They knew by its mewing that the bundle must be a kitten, a lost kitten with no family and no name.

"Poor kitty," said the sisters.

"Let him stay with us," said Lester.

"But a *cat!*" said Mother Miggs.

"Why not?" said Father Miggs.

"We can bring him up to be a good mouse. He need never find out he is really a cat. You'll see—he'll be a good thing for this family."

"Let's call him Mickey," said Lester.

And that's how Mickey Miggs found his new family and a name.

After his eyes opened he began to grow up just as mice do, eating all kinds of seeds and bugs and drinking from puddles and sleeping in a cozy pile of brother and sister mice.

Father Miggs showed him his first tomcat—at a safe distance—and warned him to "keep away from all cats and dogs and people."

Mickey saw his first mousetrap—"The most dangerous thing of all," said Mother Miggs—when they moved to the indoor nest that fall.

He was too clumsy to steal bait from traps himself, so Lester and the sisters had to share with him what they stole.

But Mickey was useful in fooling the household cat, Hazel. He practiced up on meowing, for usually, of course, he squeaked, and became clever at what he thought was imitating a cat.

He would hide in a dark corner and then, "Meow! Meow!" he'd cry. Hazel would poke around, leaving the pantry shelves unguarded while she looked for the other cat. That gave Lester and his sisters a chance to make a raid on the left-overs.

Poor Hazel! She knew she heard, even smelled, another cat, and sometimes saw cat's eyes shining in a corner. But no cat ever came out to meet her.

How could she know that Mickey didn't know he was a cat at all and that he feared Hazel as much as the mousiest mouse would!

And so Mickey Miggs grew, becoming a better mouse all the time and enjoying his life. He loved cheese, bacon, and cake crumbs. He got especially good at smelling out potato skins and led the sisters and Lester straight to them every time.

"A wholesome and uncatlike food," said Mother Miggs to Father Miggs approvingly. "Mickey is doing well." And Father Miggs said to Mother Miggs, "I told you so!"

Then one day, coming from a nap in the wastepaper basket, Mickey met the children of the house, Peggy and Paul.

"Ee-eeeeek!" Mickey squeaked in terror. He dashed along the walls of the room looking for his mousehole.

"It's a kitten!" cried Peggy, as Mickey squeezed through the hole.

"But it acts like a mouse," said Paul.

The children could not understand why the kitten had been so mouselike, but they decided to try to make friends with him.

That night as Mickey came out of his hole he nearly tripped over something lying right there in front of him. He sniffed at it. It was a dish and in the dish was something to drink.

"What is it?" asked Mickey. Lester didn't know, but timidly tried a little. "No good," he said, shaking his whiskers.

Mickey tried it, tried some more, then some more and some more and more and more—until it was all gone.

"Mmmmmmmmm!" he said. "What wonderful stuff."

"It's probably poison and you'll get sick," said Lester disgustedly. But it wasn't poison and Mickey had a lovely feeling in his stomach from drinking it. It was milk, of course. And every night that week Mickey found a saucer of milk outside that same hole. He lapped up every drop.

"He drank it, he drank it!" cried Peggy and Paul happily each morning. They began to set out a saucerful in the daytime, too.

At first Mickey would drink the milk only when he was sure Peggy and Paul were nowhere around. Soon he grew bolder and began to trust them in the room with him.

And soon he began to let them come nearer and nearer and nearer still.

Then one day he found himself scooped up and held in Peggy's arms. He didn't feel scared. He felt fine. And he felt a queer noise rumble up his back and all through him. It was Mickey's first purr.

Peggy and Paul took Mickey to a shiny glass on the wall and held him close in front of it. Mickey, who had never seen a mirror, saw a cat staring at him there, a cat in Paul's arms where he thought *he* was. He began to cry, and his cry instead of being a squeak was a mewing wail.

Finally Mickey began to understand that he was not a mouse like Lester and his sisters, but a cat like Hazel.

He stayed with Peggy and Paul that night, trying not to be afraid of his own cat-self. He still didn't quite believe it all, however, and next morning he crept back through his old hole straight to Mother Miggs.

"Am I really a cat?" he cried.

"Yes," said Mother Miggs sadly. And she told him the whole story of how he was adopted and brought up as a mouse. "We loved you and wanted you to love us," she explained. "It was the only safe and fair way to bring you up."

After talking with Mother Miggs, Mickey decided to be a cat in all ways. He now lives with Peggy and Paul, who also love him, and who can give him lots of good milk and who aren't afraid of his purr or his meow.

Mickey can't really forget his upbringing, however. He takes an old rubber mouse of Peggy's to bed with him.

He often visits the Miggses in the indoor nest, where he nibbles cheese tidbits and squeaks about old times.

And of course he sees to it that Hazel no longer prowls in the pantry at night.

"Oh, I'm so fat and stuffed from eating so much in Hazel's pantry," Father Miggs often says happily to Mother Miggs. "I always said our Mickey would be a good thing for the family—and he is!"

HOUSES

By ELSA JANE WERNER

Illustrated by TIBOR GERGELY

Houses, houses, houses!
Everyone lives in some kind of a house.
Don't you?
Maybe it is a small house on a quiet street.

Maybe it is a big apartment house
where a lot of families live.

Maybe it is a middle-sized house
in a nice middle-sized town.

Maybe it is a trailer in a trailer park.
But everyone lives in some kind of a house.
Because everyone needs a home.

"Why do people need houses?" you ask.
Well, a house keeps you dry when it rains.
Some places it rains almost every day.
There the houses may stand on stilts.

Or they may be built in trees.
Tree houses have steep roofs
so the rain slides down,
and the home inside stays dry.

A house keeps you warm in the cold.
Some places there is snow
much of the year.
Even the houses may be built
of cakes of snow.
These houses are called igloos.

In other lands,
houses may be built of mud.

A house shelters you from the wind.
It may be a warm round house of felt,
with no corners for the wind
to whistle past.

It may be a chalet with stones
on the roof,
to keep it from blowing away.

A house shelters you from the sun.
It may be a tent to keep you in the shade,
or a house with thick, cool walls.

It may be a woven hut of brush
—or of grass.
But if you live there, it is home.

Yes, wherever you live you need a house.
But what will you build it of?

If you live in a land with lots of trees,
you may build your house of wood.
It may be a cabin of round brown logs,
or a white-painted Colonial house.

It may be half-timbered,
with a steep, gabled roof,
or even a wooden gypsy cart.

If you live in a land with no tall trees,
you may build your house of clay.
You may use bricks shaped smooth
and burned hard.
You may have a house of bricks.

You may use thick adobe blocks
of clay and straw dried in the sun.
And you'll wash the adobe walls with color.
You will have a nice adobe house.

You may build your house
of the stone around you.
Some people's houses are partly caves.

Some live up on the tops of cliffs,
where no one can take them
by surprise.

Some houses of stone are castles—very old,
with towers from which to watch
the countryside.
You may build your house of solid stone.

You may build it lightly of delicate woods,
with some walls of paper
the light comes through.
If the earth should tremble
and the house fall down,
you could quickly build it up again.

You may have walls all of glass brick,
for the light comes through those, too.

Or you may have windows
from ceiling to floor,
so the sun can help warm your house.

Your house may be a boat on a river
or a sea.

It may turn its windows and
front porch to the street.

Or it may have a plain wall
on the street,
with all the friendliness inside.

You may have steel girders
inside your walls,
so you can build a house
that is very tall.
You may squeeze your house in
between two others just as tall.

Or you may set it down
in the middle of a lawn,
with space for children to play.

Yes, everybody needs a house
and home.
Which kind will you choose?

THE TWINS

The Story of Two Little Girls Who Look Alike

By RUTH *and* HAROLD SHANE

Illustrated by ELOISE WILKIN

Ann and Sue were playing in the bright early September sunshine. One was swinging and one was digging in the sandbox. But which was Ann and which was Sue?

Both were wearing blue sun suits. Both were wearing brown shoes. But it wasn't because of what they wore that they *looked* alike. It was because they were twins. Not all twins look the same, but Ann and Sue looked almost *exactly* the same.

Ann had light brown hair—like Sue's. Sue had blue eyes—like Ann's. In fact, all their friends and neighbors had trouble sometimes in telling them apart. Many, many times they got them mixed up and called Ann "Sue" and Sue "Ann." It was most confusing!

Even Mother and Daddy could not tell the twins apart when they were at the far end of the yard. To avoid calling them by the wrong name, Mother often called them together, using both names.

"Sue and Ann!" she called. "Time to change your clothes. This is the day we are going to buy new dresses for school."

When the girls were freshly washed and combed they looked even more alike, if possible. For their trip to the store they both wore red dresses, red barrettes in their hair, white socks, and black shoes.

On the way to the store, Mother said, "This time I think your dresses should be different. The teacher and the other girls and boys will find it easier to tell you apart if you don't dress always exactly the same."

"Oh, no!" Sue and Ann said together in alarm.

Sue added, "It's fun to look alike."

"Yes," said Ann. "We like to tease people. We can fool them more easily when we dress the same."

Mother said, "I should think it would be more fun if you didn't look always the same. We gave you names that didn't sound alike because it is confusing enough to have two girls the same age. Now you are really trying to confuse people. But, if that is what you want, get your clothes alike."

At the store, they chose shoes and socks that were the same, and dresses and coats and hats.

"I've seen lots of twins," said the clerk, "but never any that look just as much alike as their clothes do."

That afternoon when Ann and Sue were home, they smelled cookies baking. "Umm," said Ann. "I can tell Mrs. Wildeman is making brownies."

"Let's ask Mother if we can show her our new dresses," said Sue. "Maybe she will give us cookies."

"Of course you may," said Mother when the girls asked if they could visit their next-door neighbor. "Mrs. Wildeman will be pleased to have you call. Be careful to keep clean, though."

Sue raced upstairs. She changed her clothes much faster than Ann and in a moment Mrs. Wildeman heard a tap-tap on her screen door.

"Why, how *nice* you look, Ann—or is it Sue?" she said. "Come in and have a brownie. Tell your sister I'd love to see her dress, too."

Sue said, "Thank you for the cookie," as she darted out the door, and in a moment there was a second tap-tap at the door.

"Come in, my dear, and let me see your dress," said Mrs. Wildeman. "And do have a brownie. My, that's a lovely dress! Just like your sister's."

"Thank you," said Sue. "I must go home now."

Before long there was a third tap-tap at the door. "Hello," said Mrs. Wildeman, and went about putting sugar on her cookies.

"Don't you see anything new?" asked Ann.

"No, I don't see anything different from a moment ago," said Mrs. Wildeman.

"But I just got here," said Ann in a small voice that was by now a little sad.

"Hmmmm," said Mrs. Wildeman. "How many twins are there? I've already given *two* cookies to *two* girls with *two* new dresses—" Suddenly she stopped speaking for a moment. "Or have I seen one girl in one new dress *two* times?"

"I'm Ann," said Ann. "And this is the very first time I have been here today."

"Oh dear," said Mrs. Wildeman with a smile. "I have been fooled again. I've given two cookies to Sue and none to Ann! Here are two brownies for you, Ann—next time both of you come over together."

Soon it was Monday and time for school to start. Ann and Sue put on their new clothes and started off. They had been to kindergarten the year before and so their mother did not need to go with them. Each had a letter from school telling her that Mrs. Kramer was her new teacher.

"Well, you young ladies certainly look alike!" Mrs. Kramer said when she saw the girls. "How will I ever be able to tell which is Ann and which is Sue?"

Ann and Sue just grinned. They didn't want people to be able to tell them apart. Mrs. Kramer saw twinkles in the twins' eyes.

"First of all," she said, "we'll put you on different sides of the room. Ann can have the desk near the window. Sue, you sit at the one near the door, please."

After that Mrs. Kramer could tell which was Ann and which was Sue—except when they were on the playground or when they changed seats to tease her.

None of the boys and girls in first grade did any better than Mrs. Kramer in telling Sue and Ann apart. Pretty soon they began to call both girls "Sue-Ann." "Look at this, Sue-Ann," they would say to Sue, or, "Come play with us, Sue-Ann," they would call to Ann.

Neither Sue nor Ann liked the new nickname. They liked it even less when some of the children began to call both of them "Twin." "I don't feel like anyone at all when they call me Twin," said Sue to Ann.

"And Sue-Ann is just as bad," said Ann to Sue.

That night Sue said to Mother and Daddy at suppertime, "All the kids are calling us Sue-Ann or Twin. We don't like it."

"What did you say, Ann?" Daddy asked.

"I'm not Ann, I'm Sue," said Sue.

"There, there," said Daddy. "I thought you wanted to look alike."

"But we don't now," said Ann. "We're *two*, not *one* girl, and we *each* have a name."

"Did you ever think that you don't need to look alike?" said Mother.

"But we can't help it," said Ann. "Even with different dresses we still look alike."

"Finish your dinner and I'll show you how different you can look," said Mother. "We'll change Sue-Ann into Sue *and* Ann once and for all."

When they finished their dinner they all went upstairs to Mother's dressing table.

Mother laid out scissors and bobby pins, ribbons and barrettes. And she began to braid, to cut, to pin—to comb—to curl. In thirty minutes Sue and Ann had ten new hair-do's to choose from.

Can *you* guess which ones Sue and Ann chose?

"Now," said Mother, "wiggle into different dresses and we'll see how different our two daughters look!"

How different Sue and Ann were now!

"You don't look a bit alike!" said Daddy. And he added, with a twinkle in his eye, "But my goodness! How can we remember which has long hair and which has short? Which is Sue? Which is Ann?"

"Why, that's easy!" said the girls. "Just remember—"

"That I am Sue!" said Sue.

"And I am Ann!" said Ann.

Our look-alike twins
Have gone away.

Now two different girls
Have come to stay.

Hello, Ann!
Hello, Sue!

How lucky we are to have *both* of you!

Four Little Kittens

By KATHLEEN N. DALY

Illustrated by

ADRIANA MAZZA SAVIOZZI

Once upon a time, four kittens were born in a corner of a barn.

"I wonder what kind of cats they'll grow up to be," thought the mother cat.

She licked her four new babies proudly. They were still tiny. Their eyes were sealed shut, and they could only mew, and snuggle close to their mother's warm side.

In a few days, the kittens opened their eyes. Each day they grew a little bigger, and a little stronger. "And a great deal naughtier," thought Mother Cat, as they pounced on her twitchy tail.

"Children," she said one day, "the time has come for you to decide what kind of cats you will be."

"Tell us, tell us," mewed the kittens, "what kind of cats there are."

Mother Cat sat up straight, and half closed her green eyes, and began.

"There are Alley Cats.

"An Alley Cat is long and lean. He slinks like a shadow, sleeps where he can, eats what he finds.

"A free cat is he—no manners to mind, no washing of paws, no sheathing of claws. He does what he likes, and nobody knows but he.

"Your Uncle Tom is an Alley Cat. Many friends he has, and they make fine music at night, to the moon. His enemies are stray dogs, and turning wheels, and cold, sleety rain. He's a wild and clever cat, the Alley Cat."

"That is the life for me," said Tuff, the biggest kitten. And off he went, to be an Alley Cat, like bold Uncle Tom.

"Now Uncle Tar was a Ship's Cat," Mother Cat went on. "A splendid cat he was, with a ship for a home, and sailors for friends.

"A Ship's Cat visits seaports a thousand miles away, and talks to foreign cats, and chases foreign rats that try to come aboard.

"A brave cat is he, a jolly, roving cat, a Ship's Cat. And many are the tales your Uncle Tar could tell."

"That is the life for me," said Luff, the second kitten. And off he went, to be a Ship's Cat, like jolly Uncle Tar.

"And," said Mother Cat, "there are Farm Cats.

"I am a Farm Cat, a useful cat. I catch the mice and chase the rats, while the farmer sleeps at night.

"I live in the barn on a bed of straw—no House Cat am I.

"A Farm Cat can talk to all the animals that live on the farm. A splendid, useful, strong cat is the Farm Cat—though I say it myself."

"That is the life for me," said Ruff, the third kitten. And off he went, to be a Farm Cat, like his mother. Mother Cat purred.

Now the smallest, youngest kitten was called Muff. Muff was gentle, and playful, and pretty, and always kept her white paws clean.

Muff's mother sighed and said, "Muff, I don't think you are an Alley Cat. I don't think you are a Ship's Cat, or even a Farm Cat. I don't know what kind of cat you are."

And off went Mother Cat, to catch a nice, fat mouse for dinner.

Sadly, Muff wandered out of the barn.

She caught sight of Ruff, getting ready to spring on a great big rat. Muff shivered, and crept by as quietly as she could.

"I couldn't be a Farm Cat," said Muff, "because I'm *afraid* of big rats."

Muff wandered out of the farm and down to the village.

She saw plump little Tuff, doing his best to look lean and wild like an Alley Cat.

"Wuff, wuff," barked a little stray dog, and Tuff arched his back, and bristled his fur, and spat and hissed in his best Alley Cat way.

The little dog ran away. And so did Muff.

Down to the river she ran, and she saw Luff on a big ship in the harbor.

The sailors were busy with ropes and things, but already Luff had curled up in a place where he wouldn't be in the way. Soon Luff would be visiting cats a thousand miles away, just like Uncle Tar.

Muff waved good-by. "I wish I knew what kind of cat I am," she sighed. Then she had to run out of the way as a bicycle came by.

It began to rain, and Muff got cold and wet. She didn't like that at all, and she shook her wet paws crossly. She lay down to sleep on a lumpy pile of sacks. She didn't like that very much, either.

She was cold and hungry and cross, and when a big hand picked her up, she spat and hissed for all the world like an Alley Cat.

But the big hand put her into a big, warm pocket, and after a few more angry squawks, and a sad little mew, Muff fell asleep.

When next she opened her eyes, Muff was in a house. There were cushions and carpets and curtains. There was a warm, crackling fire.

There was a little girl with soft, gentle hands.

"Oh, what a lovely kitten," said the little girl. "Oh, I wanted a kitten so much. Now I won't be lonely any more."

The little girl gave Muff a saucer of cream.

Muff drank it all, with one white foot in the saucer to keep it steady. Then she washed her paw, and licked her whiskers.

This was *much* better than fat mice for dinner.

The little girl played with Muff. She dangled a string, and Muff jumped and pounced in her prettiest way, and the little girl laughed with delight.

Muff purred.

This was much better than running away from barking dogs, and turning wheels.

The little girl lifted Muff onto her warm lap, and stroked Muff's fur.

"Oh, it's nice to have a kitten," said the little girl.

Muff purred loudly.

This was much better than a pile of lumpy sacks, or even a bed of straw.

"This is the life for me," purred Muff. "I know what kind of cat I am. I'm a cushion and cream cat, a purring cat, a cuddlesome cat, a playful cat, a little girl's cat—I'm a House Cat!"

And so all four kittens lived happily ever after—Tuff in his alley, because he was an Alley Cat, Ruff on his farm, because he was a Farm Cat, Luff on his ship, because he was a Ship's Cat, and Muff on her cushions, in her house, with her little girl, because she was a House Cat.

THE HAPPY MAN AND HIS DUMP TRUCK

By MIRYAM

Illustrated by TIBOR GERGELY

Once upon a time there was a man who had a dump truck.

Every time he saw a friend, he would wave his hand and tip the dumper.

One day he was riding in his dump truck, singing a happy song, when he met a pig going along the road.

"Would you like a ride in my dump truck?" he asked.

"Oh, thank you!" said the pig. And he climbed into the back of the truck.

After they had gone a little way down the road, the man saw a friend.

He waved his hand merrily and tipped the dumper.

"Whee," said the pig. "What fun!" And he slid all the way down to the bottom of the dumper.

Very soon they came to a farm.

"Here is where my friends live," said the pig. "You have a nice dump truck.

"Would you please let my friends see your truck?"

"I will give them a ride in my dump truck," said the man.

So the hen and the rooster climbed into the truck.

And the duck climbed into the truck.

And the dog and the cat climbed into the truck.

And the pig climbed back into the truck, too.

And the man closed the tail gate, so they would not fall out.

And then off they went!

They went past the farm, and all the animals waved to the farmer.

The man was very happy. "They are all my friends," he said. So he waved his hand, and tipped the dumper.

The hen, the rooster, the duck, the dog, the cat, and the pig all slid down the dumper into a big heap!

The hen clucked.

The duck quacked.

The rooster crowed.

The dog barked.

The cat mewed.

And the pig said a great big grunt.

The animals were all so happy!

Then the man took them for a long ride, and drove them back to the farm.

He opened the tail gate wide and raised the dumper all the way up.

All the animals slid off the truck onto the ground.

"What a fine sliding-board," they all said.
"Thank you," said all the animals.
"Cut, cut," clucked the hen.
"Cock-a-doodle-doo," the rooster crowed.
"Quack-quack," quacked the duck.
"Bow-wow," barked the dog.

"Meow, meow," mewed the cat.
And the pig said a great big grunt.
"Oink, oink!"

The man waved his hand and tipped the dumper, and he rode off in his dump truck, singing a happy song.

My Little Golden Book About

By JANE WERNER WATSON

Illustrated by ELOISE WILKIN

God is great.
Look at the stars in the evening sky,
so many millions of miles away
that the light you see shining left its star
long, long years before you were born.

Yet even beyond the farthest star,
God knows the way.
Think of the snow-capped
mountain peaks.
Those peaks were crumbling
away with age
before the first men
lived on earth.
Yet when they were raised up
sharp and new
God was there, too.

Bend down to touch the smallest flower.
Watch the busy ant tugging at his load.
See the flash of jewels on the insect's back.
This tiny world your two hands could span,
like the oceans and mountains
and far-off stars,
God planned.

Think of our earth, spinning in space
so that now, for a day of play and work
we face the sunlight, then we turn away—
to the still, soft darkness for rest and sleep.
This, too, is God's doing.
For GOD IS GOOD.

God gives us everything we need—
shelter from cold and wind and rain,
clothes to wear and food to eat.

God gives us flowers, the songs of birds,
the laughter of brooks,
the deep song of the sea.

He sends the sunshine to make things grow,
sends in its turn the needed rain.

God makes us grow, too, with minds
and eyes to look about our wonderful world,
to see its beauty, to feel its might.

He gives us a small still voice in our hearts
to help us tell wrong from right.
God gives us hopes and wishes and dreams,
plans for our grown-up years ahead.

He gives us memories of yesterdays,
so that happy times and people we love
we can keep with us always in our hearts.
For GOD IS LOVE.

God is the love of our mother's kiss,
the warm, strong hug of our daddy's arms.

God is in all the love we feel for
playmates and family and friends.

When we're hurt or sorry or lonely or sad,
if we think of God, He is with us there.

God whispers to us in our hearts:
"Do not fear, I am here
And I love you, my dear.
Close your eyes and sleep tight
For tomorrow will be bright—
All is well, dear child.
Good night."